Gadlynn Wa

Hunt

A First Ranger of the King Story

By David L. Anderson

Illustrations by

Hugor & Hugorky Rodriguez

A GreyCastle Entertainment Production

David L. Anderson

dl.anderson@comcast.net

Special Thanks

Special thanks to all those who helped make this dream a reality!

Editor

Christian Byard

Book Layout, promotion and website design

Jerry Dreessen

Cover design layout

Ben Israelson

Book Cover and Design

Grant Kempster

Early Conceptual Idea and Designs

Ashley Fouch

Scott Figgins

Early Readers

William T. Greimes

Jay Anderson

Beta Readers

Courtney M. Privett

Ashley Fouch

Angela Figgins

Additional support

Stephen Grenley

Deanna Sarkar

Christian Doyle

Chuck Davenport

Scott Figgins

Rick Medved

Kimberly Coleman @ Seven Meadows Archery

Eric Pope:

"Wotan the fairysmasher and his likeness is copyrighted by Eric Pope with direct permission for use in this novel and artwork"

Michelle at the Lynnwood Fed. Ex store!

GreyCastle Entertainment

ISBN 978–0–578–62598–0

Printed in the U.S.A.

DEDICATION -

This book is dedicated to my Father, John Anderson, my real life hero who always encouraged me to keep writing... and also to my Mother, Shirley Anderson, who baked the best cookies ever, made from scratch with chocolate chips and love...

Stay Tuned...

BARBARIAN TERRITORIES
BARREN PEAK
OLBERT
HARLAN FOREST
DROTH
MT. GOOR
GREENSDALE
DARNELL
HALERIN
BELLWOOD
FARNAH
TWO FORKS
CASTLE VIGILANT
CASTLE VELON
MT. SHEPARD MONASTERY
Greycastle
WEST VANDORIA
FLOWING FLATS
ORDANIA
VANDORIA
TERAAL
CITY OF ST. LEON
Castle Ordania
KRAIGON heights
ALANDORA RIVER
BORDER
STENWOOD
CAUSTIN SWAMPS
COLBRIDGE
OAKWOOD ISLAND
FORT DARKMOOR
LAPAAR
HALSTOCK
RUINS
HAGARD
ISLAND OF NOZZ
THE POINT
SOUTH ISLAND
SEA OF ALANDORA
UNENDING SEAS
ALANDORA
GLAASE

PRELUDE

The moon shone brightly. Alena was so excited she could barely contain herself. Mother and Father would soon be sound asleep--Papa snoring like angels blasting trumpets to the heavens. Poor Mother, how could she deal with that?

Alena re-focused her thoughts on the task at hand. There was something about not doing what you are told, nor expected to do, that was... thrilling, even adventurous. Stealing away into the night to meet him certainly fell into that category.

This would be their third late-night meeting behind Milford's hay barn. Nothing torrid or scandalous would happen; Alena was very proper in that regard, but just being near him was enticing enough to make the risk worth any kind of disapproval or discipline if caught. Bradon was to be her betrothed someday...

she just knew it.

It wasn't a mere matter of features, captivating though they were: Dark brows accompanied his calming ebony eyes, thick black hair draped down in waves (most times in desperate need of a brush,) but it was his smile that thrilled her most. Rare, perfect, white teeth resting on a chiseled chin. Yes, Bradon's smile melted her quicker than butter on a hot pan. A special smile that he shared only with her.

A slight chill in the wind prompted Alena to reach for her shawl: a shoulder wrap that she had crafted with her Mother over the last year with great care and skill. Various shades of brown cascaded down in intricate weaves with a wide streak of pale yellow through its center. Ma said it was her best work as of yet. Ma had learned it from her Mother, and on up the line it went. It was a craft not all women came to perfect, but Alena's dexterous fingers, even in her mid-teens, proved to be the envy of those involved. She hoped Bradon would comment, then she could offer to weave him a shawl.

Alena giggled. How handsome would he look adorned in a shawl!

The townsmen would never let him live it down. Perhaps a coat. A thick winter's coat. Yes, lined with fur. Something warm, yet masculine-looking, a jacket his friends would be envious of.

She gazed out the window at the gray wisps wrapping gently around the moon. Its position in the night sky indicated it was time. He would be waiting for her.

Alena silently crept down the hallway. Her ears perked after hearing the reassuring sounds of her father's slumbering serenade. She was even granted a few snores from her Mother.

Parents certainly appreciate breathing when they sleep.

Back into her room she went. Opening her shutters, she skillfully exited out the window, straightened out her dress and began to step off the porch-

THUNK!

-a dagger lodged itself in the wooden beam directly in her path.

“You’re not going to meet him again, are you?” a shadowed figure whispered as the wiggling blade stilled.

Alena settled back into the dress she’d nearly jumped out of.

“Shhhh... you’ll wake them!”

Parents aside, if there was one thing that could ruin a delicious, deviously-crafted plan, it would be her older sister, Darna: the amateur ranger, worry-wart extraordinaire.

“And yes...yes, I am going to meet him again!” she replied.

Darna stepped out from the shadows. She wore forest green trousers and a brown tunic, wrapped in a smoky gray cloak, just like the Rangers that served the King.

“If he lays an unwanted hand on you...” Darna promised.

“He won’t!” she protested, “He is a gentleman- unlike some of the rabble you consort with!” Darna rolled her eyes. “Those are soldiers, of course they’re going to be a bit more on the

'rabble' side of things. But they have never done anything disrespectful," Darna countered as she grasped the buried dagger.

She tugged it free and felt the edge.

"Besides, if they did, they would soon regret it."

Alena's eyes widened. "On that, I believe you." She paused for a moment before continuing. "Darna, you have to believe me too. Nothing is going to happen between me and Bradon except..."

"Except?" Darna prompted.

Alena smiled, "Except hopefully a goodnight kiss."

Darna sighed and sheathed her blade. She approached her sister and calmly grabbed her shoulders. "Listen, some of the livestock from Otto's farm have disappeared, most likely wolves or a mountain lion. You have to be careful."

Alena reached in and hugged her sister.

"Of course I'll be careful. My older sister taught me how to take care of myself."

They smiled. Darna took a step toward the house, then turned back. "Go before I cough loud and wake Pa."

Alena smiled brightly and took off toward the field that lead to Milford's barn.

***

Darna watched her go, glad that she was happy, then silently retreated back into the house. She laid on her bed and said a silent prayer for Alena. Then, she fell into a fitful sleep, dreaming of being a ranger under the service of her idol, the legendary Gadlynn Wayfare.

***

After walking awhile, Alena could finally see the outline of the old barn. The backside was close to the forest line but even at night the old structure was solid and easy to distinguish. Holes had developed all along the outer walls over the years but the roof held strong. She recalled hearing Farmer Milford one time say, “As long as the hay keeps dry, why bother fix’n ‘er?” Alena smiled, thinking about the alternate plan in case it rains, cuddling in the hay. She liked the thought of that. *Are those rain clouds coming in?*

***

Bradon heard Alena approaching the other side of the barn and tried to make himself quiet. He risked a look, sticking his head around the corner. She hadn’t spotted him. How lovely she looked in the moonlight...

She was beginning to look around for him, seeming slightly concerned. He waited another moment, as long as he figured he could without risking discovery, took a deep, slow breath, and rounded the corner from the backside of the barn.

“Boo!”

Alena shrieked, stifling her yell with her hand. They looked at each other giggling, their laughter quickly evolving into a warm embrace.

“I think you rather enjoy scaring me!” Alena accused.

“Just to see you jump was worth your wrath!” He grinned,“Did you miss me?”

“You know I did!” Alena batted her crystal blue eyes, “You... miss me?” Moonlight set her straight blond hair aglow, making Bradon want to run his fingers through it to test if it was as silky soft as it looked. In Bradon’s mind she was prettier than any girl in town, including her sister Darna-and that’s saying something. But Bradon wasn’t going to let on how he truly felt...not yet.

“Well,” he stalled, “I reckon I did miss you some.” Alena responded with her best boo-boo face. Sad eyes and a pouty upper lip. It worked every time on men when she wanted her way with something. Women, for some reason, were unsympathetic to this tactic.

“Just...some?” she coaxed.

Bradon shuffled in place and willingly fell under her spell.

“Ahh... maybe more than just a little. Maybe a whole lot...” She smiled up at him, making his knees weak, but he held strong.

He pulled her in close and began to run his fingers through that gorgeous hair.

Alena did not object. She welcomed it.

Their two bodies, warmed by their embrace, were fueled by the quickening of their heartbeats. Bradon slowly tilted her head back. Moonlight illuminated the features on her face.

What a frame of beauty, he thought. A painting worthy of adorning any wall in a King's palace.

"A whole lot, Alena Deloom..." Bradon whispered.

The young lovers' faces moved close, so close they shared each other's breath. He looked intensely into her brilliant eyes and saw the princess locked in her heart, longing to be freed.

Spurred on by passion, their lips slowly joined.

A few moments later Alena interjected, "So you did miss me!" He laughed, grinning wider than ever, "Each and every moment, can you tell?"

"I can," she replied, "but I think I might like some more convincing" -

CRACK.

They turned toward the treeline in unison. It was dark in the woods, any details indistinguishable.

"What was that?" Bradon asked anxiously. He attempted to usher Alena away but she slipped her arm out of his hold.

"AAAhhh! Darna!!" Alena said, anger rising up, "I told you to leave us be!"

"Darna?" Bradon added, relieved.

"Yes. She said she was going to skin some of your flesh off with her dagger if you did anything improper."

"Did she now? Darna! Your Ranger skills are lacking!" insisted Bradon.

The beast broke through the brush like lightning through a storm cloud.

The only thought that Bradon had time for before his life ended was, Bears can't be this big. The beast's mighty paw swatted him aside. Hurled into the air, he crumpled to the ground with finality.

***

Alena's scream rose sharply into the night, but it was short-lived. The massive, brown-furred killing machine was on her in an instant. Its jaws found her, and it shook her angrily-like a thing that had forgotten hunger and, in its place, had stoked a ferocity bordering blind rage.

Alena's light left this world. A dear soul transitioned into eternity to be reacquainted with past loved ones, perhaps walking hand in hand with Bradon into the afterlife.

***

Darna darted upright, her bed covers falling off. Something was wrong, she just knew it. Still dressed, she hastily slipped on her boots, grabbed her bow and quiver of arrows, and ran out the door. In her excellent condition, it did not take long for Darna to see the barn up ahead. The cold in the air revealed the fog from her breath as she sprinted the whole way in record time.

While approaching the barn she prayed for a reply-

"Alena!... Alena!"

Dogs barked in the distance; other people were approaching.

Darna circled around to the rear of the barn and that's where she saw his body.

A dark unmoving figure lay in the grass. She ran up to it, instantly recognizing Bradon but almost lost her stomach seeing all the blood and the unnatural way his arm was folded back.

Panic seized her -

"Alena! Alena!" she desperately cried out.

There on the ground she noticed a piece of cloth. Darna's heart burst. It was a torn section of Alena's shawl. Brown lace next to pale yellow. She could hardly tell it was yellow; blood covered most of it.

Darna cried. A flow of hot tears rippled down her cheeks. Soon after, farmer Milford and his two sons showed, and with them, three howling hounds. They pulled excitedly at their leashes, beast and blood in the air stirring them into a frenzy. They banded together and attempted to track Alena through the forest, but they had no success. Even the dogs were of no help. It was as if the hellbound creature disappeared.

That evening changed not only the lives of Darna and her parents forever, but also the entire village of Greensdale where they lived. The townspeople attempted multiple hunts for this beast, but nothing came into fruition. All clues proved useless. Of course, Darna was at the forefront of every effort-

Haunted by the death of her sister. Darna vowed she would never allow herself to be idle, unprepared. Always to remain vigilant.

Always ready to hunt for it, to track it, to KILL it. Above all, she wanted her sister back. Wanted to tease her, mess with her hair, throw food at her...hug her. Yet that couldn't happen. But if not for that, there was something that she would be willing to sacrifice her life for, no matter what the means, no matter what the costs. Darna wanted one thing- just this one other thing.

Darna wanted revenge.

Chapter 1

A WISE MAN REFLECTS ON LEGEND

The following Journal is taken directly from Brother Matthew's first transcript concerning Gadlynn Wayfare as directed upon by King Gerald, Lord of Ordania and all lands east of the Alandora river.

* * *

"When legend be told and truth be sought, let the tales of history be championed with accuracy".

This commission has been placed upon me, Brother Matthew, by the most wise and noble King Gerald, ruler of the free lands of Alandora and keeper of peace (when not interfered with by King Falnar!) This King I serve willingly, of course, after my first allegiance to my heavenly Father and King.

It was soon after Gadlynn Wayfare's rise to the position of First Ranger that this duty was entrusted to me. A daunting task, dare I say, yet I reluctantly agreed.

I recall the assembly was quite impressive...

Wise leaders and elder monks gathered from near and far to assemble in Castle Ordania's magnificent meeting hall.

Peerlessly crafted white columns held firm the building's

vault while finely woven tapestries, displaying conquest of old, lined the walls between vibrant stained-glass windows. High above, the ceiling was adorned with enchanting painted scenes of the heavens, sainted angels with outstretched wings soaring in the midst of billowy clouds. It was so inspirational, it looked as if God brushed them on himself, a reminder to all where our real power comes from.

We watched as King Gerald stood upon the dais and declared to all those present, "Let the record be accurate, let the record be true. I want our histories to speak truth, not falsehoods or exaggerations."

That was his exact quote, it struck me as noble, so I penned it then and there. Unfortunately, and ironically, moments later the King would ask me to be The Historian-the keeper of these truths and histories.

With the room full of knowledgeable and competent men, the King scanned the crowd until his roving eyes landed upon my uneasy countenance. I squirmed slightly, if I recall.

"In this assembly reside many of Alandora's wisest and gifted scholars, gathered to address matters of importance and concern to our Kingdom. We also, on occasion, appoint individuals to oversee certain of these matters. One assignment I will appoint now before continuing is that of 'Royal Historian'. This position will keep records on future key events, especially those concerning Gadlynn Wayfare, our newly appointed First Ranger. I strongly feel she is gifted from the Almighty Himself."

The room reacted rather negatively at that last statement. But it bothered the King not and he continued, "So it is of utmost importance that we document future events accurately... fairly.

It is a monumental task, I know, but I have the utmost confidence that the person I choose will excel at the task even better than he himself believes".

I was impressed by his ability to act like he did not know in advance he was going to pick me. Bravo, brilliant performance!

"So, among all of you gathered today, I feel most lead towards... hmmm... let me see..."

He wasn't fooling me for a grain of time-sand...

"I think..."

That's right... scan the assembly to elevate their hopes. Choose one of them! Please!... Please??

"Brother Matthew. I feel you would be most fitted for this task".

He had me nailed to this cross days ago, I just know it!

The assembly was stunned. There were SO many more qualified than myself. Overly self-opinionated eyes filling overly adorned wardrobes of prestige turned to stare their fiery gazes my way.

I sat there quivering in my overly wrinkled humble brown robe.

"My dear Brother Matthew, will you please stand and share with us your thoughts and vision on your approach to this task?" Could we add a little backstreet tavern rum to my open wound please?

So, realizing I did not possess the power of invisibility, I transformed my face into that of a most noted and wise scholar.

Maybe I shall fool a few.

"My most noble King. I stand here humbled and also...

astounded. To be chosen over my most esteemed and more deserving comrades is..."

"Did I choose... incorrectly?"

"No, my King! It is just that I... that I am not as deserving as my surroundings..."

With a wide sweep of hands, I gestured the inclusion of my peers and superiors. I thought it looked a tad exaggerated, yet the assembly rather liked it. As long as I knew they were my superiors, the process would go a little smoother.

Without missing a beat, and as if he had anticipated my objection, the king said, "Then perhaps this is one of the reasons why I have chosen you. When one feels they are undeserving it is most likely that they are most deserving. Humility is a quality of the wise." He probably stated that accurately. Compared to these pretentious over-inflated egos surrounding me, he most definitely stated that accurately. Is it possible to have pride about your humbleness? I will have to research this later...

I bowed, perhaps deeper than I needed to. "I am your humble servant, my King."

"I have read your reports and accounts, and have found them to be well composed and most of all... accurate. Yes, you shall be well suited for this."

May as well get into this. "My pen shall be at your command, my King."

Pleased, King Gerald replied, "My Knights serve with swords, and you shall serve with ink."

Laughter. For some reason, the spectators found that amusing. If the castle were under attack, I would much rather wield a sword than a pen. Of course, my calling doesn't require the shedding of blood- just the shedding of ink.

"I am grateful, my King. Grateful to serve you and the kingdom in such a way that makes best use of my calling and my humble talents. I shall be very meticulous in my duties. With detailed, accurate accounts pertaining to events of the kingdom, including any developments concerning our newly-appointed First

Ranger, Gadlynn Wayfare."

"Well stated. So let us declare on this fine hour that Brother Matthew, esteemed Monk and servant of God, shall oversee the recording and documentation of all major kingdom events..." As if "documenting all major events" weren't enough, yet maybe I was being selfish...

"... and of those concerning First Ranger, Gadlynn Way--huh?" "My good King, might I say a word?" a voice interrupted.

It was just a matter of time. Very short time. Adviser Walmoor (nicknamed "Blabbermore") had an opinion on everything and there was no time that wasn't the right time for him to share it. Like right now, for instance.

"But of course..." the king replied, with a flicker of uncertainty.

"I would never be one to question the thoughtful deliberations of our most highly regarded King," Blabbermore jumped in with both flat feet, "yet I am left to ponder on such a use of resources for laborious documentations just for the mere Ranger girl. Yes, I am quite aware of her impressive display of ability at your games sire, yet--"

I just knew there had to be yet another yet.

"-is she so impressive as to facilitate such an unusual proclamation? Past First Rangers were equally skilled and impressive in their ascension to this prestigious position. None in this assembly today has forgotten the magnificent deeds of Talbert the Tall nor Marcus "Tiny" Redfern nor even those of our beloved, recently-departed Stephen Trushot. Why, even in my own barony there is the legendary...

"SO..."

I tried not to let a relieved sigh pass my lips. Thank you, my good King. Well-placed interruption is always welcomed.

"If," King Gerald began coolly, "I am to sift through and accentuate on the lavishness of your... proclamation: why all the bother with this Ranger?" The crowd, missing his tone, eagerly agreed. Old Blabbermore stood there smirking with a profound "smuggery". I made that word up. I feel it works rather fittingly in this case.

"And furthermore, he continued, "what has she accomplished??" The assembly concurred with one accord. Repetition of," Yes, what has she accomplished!?" was heard throughout the meeting hall.

"She is so young! And, dare I say it?" He grinned dangerously, "She is a woman!" My peers boisterously agreed, and some even applauded. Others knew better and still applauded! I held my tongue. My insightful King was dispersing bait, and he had them speared like river trout caught in a net.

"ENOUGH!"

The assembly was dead quiet. Even Blabbermore, God be praised.

"Those are fine men you referred to. Very fine men. They have served the Kingdom with utmost admiration and their service and deeds will not be forgotten. Yet," he added, heavily--and I didn't miss the significance of yet another yet, "even among those admirable men, I see in this... 'girl' unbelievable potential gifted from God himself." The King was in fine form. So impressive in his articulations and persuasion. The thin crown atop his head glimmered as he turned, visibly locking eyes with various dignitaries. I glanced over and noticed Blabbermore, head down, was warming his backside once again in his chair. That brought a smile to my lips.

"Just two short years ago she amazed an entire countryside, victorious over incredible odds.

"Even the contest itself was a measure of the miraculous! The Rangers have always chosen their successors and presented them to the King. Yet I was forced to hold a contest, a fair contest. If not for the pride and stubbornness of the Rangers that day, my hand would not have been forced to act! The bickering and accusations they leveled at one another was too much to bare!" He was very animated today. I suspect he did not foresee confrontation over such a simple appointment. I do rather dislike royal court politics.

"I am glad to say, after the departure of some ill-intentioned individuals and under her leadership, the Rangers have righted their course and have served with distinction!"

Bishop Browly suddenly stood. His massive frame supported a finely-embroidered red robe, proudly highlighted by laced gold trim on his sleeves. Numerous rolls of skin protruded from under his chin offering unique waves of movement when he conversed. It was quite amusing to watch. Around his neck lay elaborate necklaces of all sorts while his large portly fingers bore gem-filled rings signifying achievements of one kind or another. His whole large body ***radiated*** grandeur.

“My King, with such attention given to the girl Ranger, will not prestigious, high-ranking members of other factions also be, shall we say, resentful? Distinguished leaders such as General Geoffrey Barlow and loyal adviser Lauren Galvanster? Is their merit not also worthy of dictation?” The Bishop quickly gazed upon Lauren Galvanster, who was also in attendance, and offered a pompous nod. The good adviser lowered his head, uncomfortable with both the unwanted attention *and* example.

The King responded, “Perhaps we can even include yourself in that mention, my dear Bishop? You, good sir, are quite an established participant of the court and a fine ambassador for the Church.”

Browly snorted, “Boasting is a trait for the unsure my King, those of low self-esteem. They build upon their shallow confidence with desired praise. I do not seek the admiration of others, only that of my heavenly Father whom I so humbly serve. YET!"

Oh yes... I saw that one coming.

"Many volumes could be filled with the trials and hardships I had to endure through my ascension to Bishop. And even now, many accounts and chronicles could be noted dealing with the day-to-day activities I suffer through... for the sake of my position."

"And those activities- so elegantly brought to our attention-" the king replied, without a hint of annoyance I was cultivating, "should perhaps be handled by inner Church leadership and not that of the kingdom. Yet, please... let the record state the appreciation we hold for our noble and most observant Bishop Browly."

"I am here to humbly serve, my King. I shall immediately compose an inquiry into the matter with my superiors. Your wisdom is legendary and all of Ordania is at your service."

With that, King Gerald obliged with a nod of his head and a warm smile. I am quite sure I heard someone in the assembly mutter, "Be seated already!" to our beloved Bishop. Then again, that could have been the demands of my inner thoughts and not actually heard.

What followed soon after were the mundane formalities

concluding a kingdom affairs meeting. The King thanked everyone for their attendance and insight, there was slight applause, then all rose and began to congratulate one another. Whether their congratulations were geared towards their meeting contributions or their ability to stay awake was, in my mind, worthy of debate.

I will be the first to admit that- with the exception of a few gathered- those in attendance served the realm faithfully and were well-intentioned. Some even found their way over to congratulate me on my new, elevated position. Promotion or DEmotion? Only time will determine that one. The congregation was beginning to thin and only the King remained crowded. He was always crowded. He stood among them: approachable, yet wisely deflecting unwanted attempts at policy. The gathered well-wishers and dignitaries all hoped to leave a lasting impression, yet were, in all likelihood, well short of the mark.

I stood there watching him and could not help but marvel.

His blackened leathered tunic laced with green trim, accented well with the fur in the center. Black velvet trousers were tucked into dark leathered boots. Most likely his riding boots. He preferred comfort rather than the elaborate shoes all the aristocrats wore. In the whole of his attire, there wasn't much in the ways of gems or gold. It wasn't necessary for him, nor welcomed. His persona did not require artificial embellishments; he preferred to portray strength and nobility through his deeds, not through the haughty display of wealth and position. He was a benevolent King, yet also a Warrior King and even though I am considered an ambassador for the Church, with certain separations, I willingly serve him. I also adore him and am proud (in all humbleness of course) to call him friend. King Gerald was just what the kingdom needed at this precarious time, with the malevolent ambitions of Falnar and Grey Castle to the west. A leader whose charisma and goodness inspired all free people desiring prosperity and peace, giving them hope to persevere. I could write volumes on this man, and maybe someday I shall. For now, I will stand back and admire.

Time soon dispersed the crowd and, finally alone, the King found his way over to me. I was curious to hear his "kingly" exposition of his sudden revelation of my SO-called elevated position (or burden? I get the two mixed-up at times).

"My dear Brother Matthew, why it is a special day for you, is it not?" said the King, with a bit too much of a grin if you ask me.

"Whatever do you mean, my wise King?"

I could play along with this.

"Your prestigious advancement, of course! The Kingdom is forever grateful for your service..." King Gerald added helpfully.

"Oh!" I gasped, summoning up my best theatrics, "You

mean my new position?"

"Yes!"

"My new position, where I will never have a free moment to myself nor read any more of the many volumes I have desired for years?"

"Yes..." he replied expectantly, without a hint of the uncertainty that I'd hoped to hear.

"My prestigious new position of having to retrieve vital information from a Ranger girl whom I would be fortunate to get a 'Hello' from?" My good King just stood there basking in my admiration of his decision. I deflated further.

"The new position," I pleaded, "where I could very well find myself traveling abroad into unfriendly lands and precarious situations? Did--did I mention my feet blister easily?"

"It is most fortuitous then, that you are also a master healer!"

"Ahhh..." I spun in frustration, looking up at those blasted angels, free and gloating. "I was so content with my books, my wine sampling, and... and the occasional meetings where I shared my little pearls of wisdom…"

"You may still share your pearls of wisdom," he said with a bemused chuckle, "after, of course, you are finished with your documentations."

I quickly looked around to assure myself that we were alone and continued my self-righteous rant. “My wrists: look at them! You can already see the scarring from the chains shackled about them!” The King could not help but smile at my drama. “Oh please continue. I rather enjoy this.”

“I will be a prisoner bound to my writing table with nothing but uninteresting, half-filled volumes to show for my efforts! And patches! Patches of ink will stain my feeble hands as a badge of shame!”

“Ink washes out, most of the time...”

I pleaded my case, yet knew it was fruitless. When the King makes up his mind, he never waivers.

“Could you not have chosen Lauren Galvanster or one of the many other advisers? Or perhaps one of the young acolytes, they are both strong in mind and body! They...they would leap at the chance to serve you in such a way! Why even Blabbermore would suffice!

Dead silence.

“But I chose you...”

Tell me, how was I supposed to respond to that? I let out an audible sigh and relented.

“My King. I will do your bidding, no matter what you choose, it is just that...”

"Matthew--my dear friend--you will do fine! I am sure someday you will look back with fondness on all that you partake in." It was more fear of the future than reminiscing with fondness that concerned me.

"Yes, I am very aware that you will be placed out of your comfort at times, if there is need to travel. I am also very aware you will on occasion toil diligently late into the night," King Gerald conceded, "Yet, I am also quite sure you will feel satisfaction from a job well done. The recording of our kingdom's histories will be well served under your supervision. And I will also send assistants to help you when needed. My dearest of friends, you will still find time for your personal pleasures, I assure you. Just not as often is all."

As humans we easily get accustomed to routine. I am no exception. Interference with regular and expected course of actions leaves one feeling vulnerable to the whims of an uncertain future.

I so dislike change.

...

Fine.

"I do rather feel I have a talent in this area," I admitted, "unlike some of the others in attendance today."

"You are skilled with both ink and mind."

"Though I dislike traveling I am sure my legs will grow

accustomed. My feet eventually."

“Your blisters will soon callous, trust me on this. I was once a young soldier who marched frequently.”

“I do remember your joy when Captain Ainesworth promoted you to cavalry. Your Father would not have had anything to do with that I suppose?”

“Well... perhaps, if one was to ask for an honest account.” He offered a smile.

“There is no need to bring up the benefits of being a King’s son is there?”

We both laughed. I so enjoy his company. It is seldom that I am able to speak to him alone. Always engaged in kingdom affairs or with his loving Queen and family, it was refreshing to converse with him like days gone past, one friend to another. So in my mind it was settled then and there. I will arise to this new challenge and make the most of it, for my God and for the good of the kingdom, yet also for my good friend who asks this of me. I do not...I will not disappoint him. He is my King.

Though, I will most certainly need some advice on the Ranger girl.

“My King, may I ask of you some advice? How shall I go about acquiring accounts and documentations with the Ranger Girl? She is quite a lone wolf; my company will be ***most*** unwelcome...”

"Lone wolf, yes- she is that. It seems the extremely gifted are either crowd seekers or seekers of solitude. Gadlynn, and even you, my friend, are never one for the praises of men. A rather noble quality I admire."

"Just give me a goblet of wine and a good book, and I am at peace," I offered.

The King smiled fondly in agreement at that and continued.

"I will encourage her to become accustomed to sharing her accounts and at least try to be more open. Even though I know in her heart that she will dislike this notion, she will comply.

Gadlynn is very loyal to my service. Now keep in mind dear Brother: there will be some excursions that she will go on alone or accompanied by fellow Rangers. She will share her statement on those ventures afterwards. On those that are not as perilous, I will have you accompany her."

"As you wish my King. My King, since we are here conversing in private, might I get your opinion on another matter?" I just had to ask him this. I needed to truly believe that he believed.

"But of course..." he said expectantly.

"I hate to belabor a point, yet as the good Bishop and Adviser Walmore stated: why all this attention for her? Is she really that special?"

The King smiled and shook his head in disbelief. "They

most certainly made a ruckus earlier over such a small appointment, did they not?"

I grimaced in agreement. They did make quite a stir. Their reasonings most likely born of petty jealousy.

I do remember the next moment vividly: King Gerald looked me straight in the eye and said with complete certainty, "Why? She is directly blessed from God."

"Are we not all blessed by our Heavenly Father in one fashion or another?" I countered gently.

"We are" he agreed. "Yet, her blessings are gifts of extraordinary measure. It is as if God himself singled her out for a divine purpose or, more accurately, a divine destiny." He truly believed what he was saying. I could see it. This reassured me in the new task I would be undertaking. It also gave me contentment knowing that our Heavenly Father had a hand in this (me being his servant and all.)

The King paused and I could see him reflect.

"Soon after the ceremony of appointing our new First Ranger, Gadlynn and a few other rangers went hunting. I kept this from being public, but I went with them. I was intrigued and saw this as a unique opportunity to learn more about her. I also wanted to be reminded why she won the games and why we appointed her First Ranger. My dear Brother, she did not disappoint." He shook his head slightly in amazement, his thin crown scattering light to various areas in the room.

"Marcos Redfern calls her a 'prodigy'. I most certainly agree. You should have seen her, Matthew! The forest was like her home. She moved through the wilds like a mountain cat, barely making a sound and covering great distances. We could hardly keep up! She used her nose to track the scent of a stag and in moments, with one incredible shot, she struck. At our midday meal we marveled at her knowledge of tracking and various other skills."

"Let me guess," I interrupted, "you had venison for lunch?"

"In abundance!" the King laughed merrily, "We packed the rest out and the other Rangers shared it with their families. It was an impressive haul! When she left, they were all as inspired as I was, and as a group we agreed it was a very wise choice appointing her. She has unmeasured potential, Brother Matthew. A true gift from our Lord."

"Has she acknowledged these are gifts... gifts from the divine?"

"Gadlynn realizes that she has unique talents and abilities, yet does not credit God, nor anyone, for that matter, which I find ironic. It is obvious to you and I where her gifts come from, yet she does not believe."

"I will pray for her."

"As will I. She is fiercely loyal to our cause. A true ally in the fight for that which is just. Remember, good Brother: she is young and finding her way in the world. I am sure that with time and experience, Gadlynn will begin to understand God's plan and begin to think of Him with more... reverence."

"I am certain she will. All in time... all in good time."

"Now if you shall excuse me, I have a beautiful Queen awaiting my company. Apparently our Felese was rather uncordial to one of the ambassadors' daughters."

"Yet another lecture? I must say, she does take after you…"

"The Queen reminds me of that very thing quite often!" We shared some laughter and pleasantries, and then he departed. It did warm my heart to converse with him. When we were younger, we were the best of friends. Mischief and adventures were the norm, and far too often the young Prince and I received our own lecturing from his father, King Leonard. May God rest his soul. A loving King, he was.

I began to walk back to my humble cottage, where I soon shelved my reminiscing in favor of some hot wine and a good book.

Tomorrow I shall take inventory on materials and other supplies I shall need to commence my new duties: extra scrolls, quills and ink, page binders and such. Also, I shall look through my belongings and prepare a quick travel bag full of all necessities to help facilitate any abrupt departures- with this Ranger, probably the norm. It would be best that I am prepared, just in case. Oh, I so dislike traveling. Did I mention my feet blister easily?

Chapter 2

A NEW JOURNEY BEGINS

A few weeks after my so-called promotion, Gadlynn returned from heading up a scouting expedition. They had been gone for 3 weeks, through both good and foul weather, observing key borders and tracking King Falnar's troop movements. Upon their return, Adviser Galvanster shared that nothing noteworthy was reported, a few skirmishes and some complaints from villagers over well rights. The normality of reporting that any kingdom would welcome: all is running smoothly. Having made their reports, the patrol would receive a few days rest before resuming normal duties.

Now was the perfect opportunity to visit Gadlynn.

She was not to travel too far from the castle. Being First Ranger means you give up certain liberties at most times and, when not on assignment, are always accessible to the King and council.

I must say, waiting upon her arrival gave me time to think, to ponder on how to best approach her. From past encounters, though quite brief, I had found her quite UNapproachable.

She was not one for casual chat or social gatherings. It was obvious Gadlynn had built up walls, to protect her from what? I am not sure. Perhaps someday I will find out. Yet if I am to succeed in documenting in detail, as the King would have me do, I will have to somehow scale those walls...or at least find a doorway in.

I gathered my walking staff and a few necessities any monk of worth would carry: water, a small loaf, parchment, ink and a few scriptures to philosophize over if a setting allowed.

I said a quick prayer before setting out. I am a Monk, you know, and I find prayer- both long winded or short- to be a wonderful way of setting your bearing, especially before a meeting of this importance.

"Heavenly Father, grant your humble servant wisdom and insight to go about the King's business in the most proficient manner. Help me to find ways when there are none and to see clearly when the way is cloudy."

There, that should about do it. With staff in hand and God as my guide, I set out.

The clouds were not willing to part to let the sun participate in the day's event, but at least it was not raining. I rather dislike the rain. Though a natural necessity, rain magnifies an already dark day with the unfortunate combination of water and dirt. Resulting in mud.

Grant me sunshine oh Lord!

It began to rain. I see this will be a "character-building" kind of day.

I made on the best I could, regardless.

Now finding a Ranger in the wilds is about as easy as finding a small piece of golden straw in a haystack, yet fortune had shined on me. In the village where I live, I happened across Third Ranger Flynn: a lanky, muscled young man, blessed with a chiseled jaw and a disarming smile.

Flynn wore hunter greens and browns with various weaponry attached. Hard to spot in a forest and lethal, just the way a Ranger would have it. The young man mentioned he had conversations with Gadlynn recently and that I would most likely find her near the abandoned Castle Teraal. A place said to be haunted. She would enjoy her solitude there, that is for certain. No visitors except the occasional ghost. Or monk.

(Hopefully no ghost monk!) I thanked Flynn and was soon on my way. A long walk was in store so I had best be at it.

I would prefer not to visit Castle Teraal on this day, or any day, yet duty called and the travel would soon pass. At least the rain let up!

This is when the fog rolled in.

Definitely a character-building kind of day.

Through the thick wilderness, I toiled on. In the outskirts of the Teraal forest, I found the path that led to the old castle. I cautiously walked on, soon deep in the wild, my senses on their highest degree of alert. Tree limbs cut through mist, adding to the eerie sense of isolation. I heard no animals. I heard no birds. And yes, I admit, I was a little spooked, but the remains of Castle Teraal rested somewhere at the end of this path and I must proceed forward.

Castle Teraal had thrived centuries ago. I had read that the Teraal family made well by providing timber and high-crafted wood furniture throughout all of Alandora. Built atop a large hillside, it overlooked the Teraal Forest, and on clear days you could even see Castle Ordania, where our King resides. The castle would still flourish to this day if not for the relentless barbarian attacks that eventually brought the ruin and extinction of the Teraal family.

Unfortunately, the king of that day arrived too late, only to find the remains. Time then took over, eroding the keep into broken walls and neglected structures. Only grass and wildflowers grow there now. That and tales of ghosts.

Chapter 3

SAVED BY A STONE

With Castle Teraal rumored haunted, it would certainly make sense that the surrounding forest would be, too. This logic seemed quite justified. I don't believe in ghosts, yet at the moment I find myself vulnerable to being persuaded.

Did I just hear a howl?

My imagination seems eager to be manipulated by this forest. I must not give in!

AAAOOOOOWWWWW!!!

I most definitely heard a howl. My early morning walk soon turned into a run. I scanned about, looking for safe refuge, yet there was none. The tree bases were all lined with thick, wet moss. There was no way an out-of-shape monk could traverse those to reach the underlying branches.

The Castle ahead was bound to have a few high places among the broken-down walls- and hopefully one well-armed Ranger girl.

This would be my goal.

Blindly following a path through thick fog, I ran as fast as my robe would allow. Earlier, I prayed for God's wisdom. Now I pray for God's speed. "God-speed," I rather like that. I will have to note that later.

My legs ached and my lungs burned; still I ran on. I heard the wolf howls closer, this inspired additional speed. King Gerald, if only you can see what I am going through for you? Perhaps I am being selfish.

With the chase at full speed, there was a sudden clearing with an ascending path. With hope, I spurred on. Did you know that running uphill is harder than on the flats? I soon recognized this by almost falling over dead from exhaustion.

It was then that I heard it: the slapping of their paws. The wolves were almost upon their prey. I stumbled, got up, and ran on. Soon, I was able to see the outline of broken castle walls.

Alas! My goal is so ever near. Yet for naught; it is quite easy to outrun holy-men, I am a fine example of this.

Instead of being taken from behind, I turned to face my attackers with staff in hand. The lead wolf bore down on me with ferocity. Snarling, it leaped, ravenous muscled fur, airborne with one desire: monk stew.

I braced for the impact. KARACK!!

A large stone pounded against the beast and sent it hurtling sideways. It was immediately followed by another stone to the hindquarters.

YEELLPP!

Bruised and aching, the leader retreated to the company of the pack, which gathered about. I was very shaken, yet arose instantly and sought refuge by clumsily climbing a high section of broken castle wall.

Stones kept getting launched from somewhere out of the fog, thrown accurately like arrows. They landed their targets with great impact and precision. After many stinging blows, and to my utmost gratitude, the pack retreated back into the forest. Not long afterward, a good distance away, howls were heard as they sought out easier prey that would not offer so many bruises.

They were spared an unpleasant meal of monk that morning. Good for them, I say. It wouldn't do to have a pack of forest wolves with agitated stomachs on my account.

I looked about for the source of the stones, and in this fog, even though it was dissipating, could see none.

"Hello? Good morning, stone thrower, are you there?" No reply. I crawled down off of the wall and continued to look for my savior.

"Over this way, Monk," came a call, eventually-embarrassed on my account, or amused, I couldn't readily tell.

"Ahh! Very good! I'll be there momentarily."

I proceeded forward in what I hoped was the direction of

the reply. The mist was receding as I felt along broken-down walls and stepped over numerous piles of rubble. I thoroughly surveyed my surroundings with no results except eye strain.

"Look toward the heavens, as men of your faith tend to do..."

Oh my, that's quite amusing. I did say I was looking for my savior, after all. Very well.

Following the voice upwards, I found my prize. High up on what must have been a lookout tower, waving an apple, she sat, legs dangling over the edge of a wooden platform. How she threw those stones and climbed up there so quickly was beyond my comprehension. A good portion of wall had eroded away, exposing three different levels. Of course, she was on the top section.

"I suppose if we are to converse, I will have to climb all the way up to where you sit?"

"You could walk back through the forest and wait for me in the village," she said, her voice carrying a fascinating mix of indifference and accusation.

Oh my...oh my indeed.

"Just so you are aware," I countered." this will be the second time in one day that I have risked my life for our King!"

"Sounds like you're a Ranger."

She had a point.

Chapter 4

INTRODUCTIONS AND AGREEMENTS

I laid my staff aside and proceeded to the base of the broken tower wall. Inside me lurked a heavy, sinking feeling, like I was about to participate in my own demise: to slowly witness the gruesome results when an unappreciated monk slips and falls from great heights! But alas, I reminded myself I was not here for my own wellbeing but for that of the kingdom. I can be such a dedicated servant at times- dedicated and humble.

From the very first handhold and foot placement on slick stone, my attempts were challenged. Have you ever tried to climb dilapidated structures with robes on, or run from half-starved wolves for that matter? No easy feat I assure you! And did I mention I was afraid of heights? I was not born with the beloved wings of angels, unfortunately.

God grant me surety of foot! Onward, for my king.

It went far better than first imagined. After three slips and four partial falls and nearly suffering from a massive seized heart due solely to fear of falling to my death, I somehow managed to position myself upon the wooden planks of the platform.

Sitting, catching my breath, I leaned against the back wall.

"You smell of perspiration and fear."

Accurate... blunt, but accurate. I was not quite sure how to respond. In between gulps of air I managed to say, "Thank you. By the way, I appreciate you not lending me a helping hand upon reaching the summit here. It is so much more rewarding to sweat and grasp for every measure of real estate with one's life dangling from a precipice."

"Our King did not mention that about you."

"And what would that be, my lack of athleticism?"

"No. The sarcasm in your speech."

"It is a gift, it flows through me naturally."

Since this was our first "official" meeting of what would be a long journey ahead, I quickly concluded to initiate introductory formalities.

"I offer my sincere greetings. I am Brother Matthew, religious council to our beloved king, and you are Gadlynn Wayfare, I presume?"

She nodded.

At last, I had found the object of my promotion, or perhaps, "demotion" is better suited, time will tell. God help me.

I tactfully examined her as I recovered from the climb. She wore your typical Ranger garb: a forest-colored tunic and dark pants cinched tight with a black, sturdy leather belt which held various knives and pouches. A dark green cape covered her backside. On the platform, laying to her left, an impressive looking recurve bow, at least from what I can tell. Next to the bow, a quiver full of multi-colored feathered arrows. A strong, angular face matched well with her long, straight flowing brown hair. If I was a young Knight or Ranger, I would find her attractive, in a rugged sort of way.

She continued to dangle her legs over the platform admiring the view. I attempted to send her a message mentally, "*Can you please step back from the ledge, young lady*?" So, one of the gifts she does *not* have is mind-reading, I'll note that later. I chuckled to myself. Finally able to breathe again, I spoke up.

"I dare say, that was you who threw the stones, correct?"

"Correct," she repeated, and I almost wondered if she was making fun of me.

"How did you manage to throw them from up here?"

"I was not up here then."

I had to pause and ponder that. It did not seem humanly possible to be able to launch a barrage of rocks, then climb up to these heights. She must possess wings. I will ask her that very thing later.

"Oh, I see. I am surprised you chose stones over arrows, what if you had missed?"

“I wanted to discourage- not extinguish- the creatures. Are you in the market for a new wolf-skin robe, monk?”

I immediately- and against my will, I might add- imagined myself in the belly of one of those beasts. A new robe, indeed! I shall need to empty my entire wineskin to quench that unpleasant thought.

“Not at the moment. Yet allow me to say with all sincerity, I do so appreciate your accuracy.

Thank you for saving me…”

She nodded, accepting my gratitude with the gracefulness of a rock wall.

I joined her in silence.

After a spell, I understood why she had chosen this spot. The view from here was stunning, even on my shaky legs. The fog was parting, revealing vast stretches of forest, and far to the south you could see partial glimpses of sun reflecting on sections of Castle Ordania. Yes... yes indeed, it would be nice to be a bird, except for the heights part, of course.

I looked about me, eyeing the dilapidated structures, broken moss-covered blocks and the history of what must have been here at this "haunted" castle. It was sobering, thinking on what was.

I then remembered a poem:

* * *

"Kingdoms rise, kingdoms fall.

* * *

They stand proud, these castle walls,

* * *

Wind and time, blood and bone -

* * *

What tales abide, in the memory of stone?"

* * *

"Sir Archibald Taylor, Poems of Life, Death and Inspiration," said Gadlynn.

"Well done! You are educated?"

"Most Rangers can read and write. I was schooled by

monks near my village where I was raised."

"Impressive..."

Now was the time, if any, to tell of my reasons for coming and tracking her down.

Her being educated may allow me to philosophize with her some, yet I think I shall try the straight forward approach.

"Gadlynn, do you know why I am here?"

Her hair fell to both sides of her face as she looked to the ground momentarily. She then turned and looked me straight in the eyes.

"I'm to be documented. Though I like it not."

Yes, this young woman did have some walls around her.

My turn to nod. "Understood. If I may, I believe the King's reasoning is similar, at least metaphorically, to the poem I just quoted. He does not wish for your story, your history, to become like this castle, its legends lost in the memory of stone."

She looked away. Very distant.

"Why does the King feel I am worth going through all this trouble? I would rather do what I am called to do and be left to myself."

"Both you and I would rather not bother with some of the tasks we are called to do, but our positions demand certain responsibilities. You would like to be near your family and spend time hunting and tracking in the forest, and I would much rather be in my humble cottage sipping mulled wine and reading books."

"Yet, we must answer our 'higher calling'." She nearly spat the words.

"Correct," I said patiently. "Though, at times we like it not, we must be obedient. God will give us strength."

Gadlynn bristled at this. "I, for one, never asked for this higher calling or these gifts. Nor to have some monk meddling around attempting to scribe my every move."

She turned, looked straight into my eyes and bluntly stated, "I'm to be documented. Though I like it not. I warn you, monk, this road will not be easy. Your presence will be a burden to me. You will keep you distance when I say so, understood?"

She is not one for mincing words I see.

"Agreed. I shall do my task with the least amount of distractions possible."

And the least amount of peril, God be willing!

She nodded and returned to the view. Some would say she was cold or aloof; I would gamble to say, more focused and cautious. It will take some doing to work my way into her world. With time, I do hope she will trust or be comfortable enough with me to share her inner thoughts. That is where the true heart of this tale –her tale- lies.

And that shall be my goal. In due time, of course.

"I am glad we have had this time to share our thoughts. I look for-"

"I do not. Yet we are both bound by duty and I shall tolerate it... for my King. As for now, I must return to my quarters and check in with my men."

Without a second thought or comment, she grabbed her things and shimmied down the tower. She made it look rather easy. I marveled at her grace and then realized how I would appreciate her company on our way back through the forest. Especially if those wolves decided to return. This prompted immediate action on my part.

"Gadlynn!"

She turned my way with a blank stare.

"I would so appreciate if I might accompany you back through the forest?"

"Then hurry down and let's go," she said levelly.

I descended as best as a monk's constrictive robe would allow, yet I am happy to report only scraping my shins thrice this time around. Impressive! Tomorrow I shall wear those bruises proudly.

For today, great strides were made in following my King's orders- at least a start.

Soon, with staff in hand, I was walking alongside her.

“I certainly would like to be with you, if, by chance, we have a second meeting with that pack.”

“It is very unusual for them to be this close to the castle,” Gadlynn admitted.

She then felt the air with her nose, as if smelling their scent or sensing their presence, it was hard to tell.

“They have retreated deeper into the forest,” she said eventually.

I was not convinced she somehow knew of their position, yet *she* was and it was good news nonetheless.

“That’s a relief. That was the closest to being a main course I have ever been.”

“I hear Monk is chewy and full of gristle. They would have just spit you out.”

“What?... ahhh...”

I do believe she just made an attempt at humor. Chewy and full of gristle, really! Spit me out, would they? They would be coming back for seconds, they would.

Did I just see her smirking? A small crack just developed in that wall of hers.

This was a good start- a good start, indeed.

Chapter 5

A FIRST ASSIGNMENT FROM THE KING

We arrived safely back at the village later in the afternoon and parted ways. It was agreed that we would have an occasional meal together and start documenting Gadlynn's rise to the position of First Ranger (an incredible achievement, if you ask me).

Accurate accounting of that event would be necessary to diminish any false rumors, some of which had already begun to spread.

"Let the tales of history be championed with accuracy." I have to keep reminding myself of this commission and see it through as best as humanly possible.

A few days after my encounter with the wolves and, in particular, the lone wolf Ranger, I received word that the King wished to see me. I had just finished scribing, in detail, the Castle Teraal meeting with Gadlynn, so the timing was impeccable.

After washing my face, and other bits of grooming, I gave my robe a hearty sniff and was pleased to find that it passed the scent-test. Normally monks of my order own two robes: one for everyday use, and the other for more special occasions, like

Church gatherings and important social events. The main, everyday robe tends to soil and dirty easily, making brown a most appropriate color.

Right now most would think, "Would seeing the King not be an important event?" It would indeed, yet I know this King so well, and see him so frequently, that he would prefer to see me in my commons. It tells him that I am working hard at the task at hand, with no time for frivolous refinements.

My staff and I set off to the castle. After two turns of the hour glass I would meet with him and discover the meaning of his inquiry.

I hope everything is in order. Running a kingdom has good times and, unfortunately, bad times. I anticipate the King is curious about our first meeting and how Gadlynn responded.

Hopefully that is the bulk of it and nothing horrific like our kingdom suddenly being at war or an attempted revolution. It would be best that I adhere to the King's high standards and keep my wits plenty sharp.

God grant me perspective!

With the sun on my back, I arrived at the Castle. Two guards quickly ushered me into a foyer next to the meeting room, where I was rather surprised to find Gadlynn standing there.

She nodded. I nodded. I wanted to say, "Good morning,

Gadlynn, how is your day faring?" But it was clear that my enthusiasm would not have been returned. Here, again, was the nodding wall.

One of the King's personal guard then marched up, saving us from further awkwardness.

"The King will see you now." He gestured to both of us, so we followed him in.

Like any of the King's venues, the meeting room was impressive.

A massive, finely carved table stood proudly in the center, accompanied by elaborately-crafted matching chairs with red felt lining- chairs that I am positive are a great deal more comfortable than what I possess. Handsomely framed pictures lined the walls, elegant reminders of the importance of the kingdom and its histories.

The King sat at one end of the table, and I was pleased to see Adviser Lauren Galvanster immediately to his right.

He waved us in and seated us close.

"Ah! My morning is blessed. Good to see the both of you. Please, take your seats here and let's discuss a few matters at hand, shall we?"

"Certainly, my King," agreed Gadlynn.

"Thank you, my King," I responded. "We are blessed too. A

fine morning it is!"

We settled in- a little apprehensive, I must add. Anytime the King wants to meet for discussions, imaginations tend to wander in anticipation of the worst.

Gadlynn sat upright and rigid, her face stoic and focused.

"Of course you all know Adviser Galvanster..." The King motioned.

"Of course, blessed morning to you, Lauren," I acknowledged.

"Greetings..." offered Gadlynn, a bit woodenly.

"And to you also, Brother Matthew, Gadlynn," Galvanster returned.

The King looked at us both and quickly spoke.

“Would you care for some wine or refreshment?”

We both declined.

“Very well. So, how fares the new task at hand? Any progress being made?” he asked expectantly.

Gadlynn was obviously feeling less talkative than I, so I took the lead.

“It goes well. A few days back, we had our initial meeting, and since then we have agreed to meet for an occasional meal to gather notes which I can later put to ink.

“Excellent!” King Gerald said approvingly. “It is important that we get our histories correct. So often we look to the past for guidance, on some matter or another, and many times come across inadequate writings that one would question the authenticity of.

It may seem a humble thing, your work with ink, but I feel your task is the Lord’s work and will serve this kingdom long after us.”

“Thank you, my King. I will send over copies as soon as they are available.”

“I look forward to it. Yet now, there is another reason I have assembled this fine company. I would have the both of you venture forth on a small quest for me...”

A quest, hmmmm... sounds like traveling is in store. I

simply must get my boots fitted properly. I can already hear the complaints of my feet!

“Certainly,” said Gadlynn, her enthusiasm returning, “What would my King have me... us, accomplish?”

“This sounds important...” I added warily.

“The fate of the kingdom is certainly not at stake,” King Gerald reassured, “but it is important nonetheless. It has come to our attention that Baron Arlo, of the village Greensdale, might h ave in his possession a particular item which we would like to purchase from him. To be more precise: an artifact of some sorts, crafted of God’s Ore.

The mention of God’s Ore made us all pause. I knew some of its history, but it was a subject I could stand to learn a great deal more on.

“God’s Ore?” I asked, “Are you certain?”

“Not entirely, yet we have our suspicions,” said the King, with concern. “We have heard accounts describing the villagers as overly infatuated with Baron Arlo’s success, and never having a complaint or negative word to say. Almost that of worship.”

“Even the most well-intentioned leader has dissenters,” supplied Lauren. “All we have to do is look in this very room at our own King: Ever noble and just, still your reign is constantly questioned and challenged. No, this, I am afraid, is unnatural.”

"I certainly must talk to whoever oversees the treasury and request an increase for you, Adviser Lauren," the King jested.

"I do oversee the treasury, my Lord."

"Precisely!"

Everyone laughed except our focused Ranger, who pressed on, "Any inquiries if it be a bracelet, necklace or ring?"

"The truth is, we are not sure. But reports have come in from various sources- some quite valid- that a necklace designed and fashioned after the style of old Andaar is always seen about his neck."

"So you need us to somehow investigate the rumor's validity," I considered, "and if proven true, diplomatically convince Baron Arlo to give it to us?"

"Correct. Yet we will purchase it. We will provide you with a fair amount of gold."

I felt my brow furrowing. "Certainly, if he wanted to sell it, a lord from outside of Ordania would offer far more than our reward. These items are very rare; their magical properties fetch extraordinary prices."

"Again correct. This needs to be handled... delicately."

"Why would he not be able to keep it?" asked Gadlynn.

"It is true," spoke Adviser Galvanster, "other lords throughout Alandora possess jewelry made with God's Ore. But the difference is that we know what they have, and we know them to be well protected- and more importantly, not abused."

"We must do our very best," the King intoned, "to prevent items with these powers from falling into Falnar's hands. Keeping him and his Witch Queen from any additional advantage is extremely important to the kingdom."

"And also, if I may," added Lauren, "it is not fair to Baron Arlo's subjects that he has such a hold over them. It looks as if this ornament carries the gift of charisma or maybe even persuasion."

"He must lead them on his own accord," King Gerald agreed. "Not with the assistance of any magical manipulations. If he does have ownership, it is unlawful without authorization. Yet we need diplomacy here, not removal by force. With Falnar on the move, the last thing we need is a dissenting barony so close to the border or yet another enchanted item slipping into the Witch Queen's control."

"Especially one with the power of persuasion," scowled Lauren. "they could bewitch surrounding allies into breaking the peace with Ordania."

"I now understand your emphasis on diplomacy," I said. "Gadlynn carries the prestige of First Ranger, so the King's concern on this matter will indirectly be perceived. I represent the spiritual side of the kingdom and hopefully appeal to his good nature, in a non-threatening manner, of course."

"Yes," affirmed the King. "Sending a squad of infantry would immediately be seen as a threat. And as we're not entirely certain it is God's Ore he possesses, discretion is in order.

Gadlynn, any comments?"

Gadlynn considered silently for a moment before uncorking the question that had apparently been bubbling up in both of us since the mention of "God's Ore".

"Yes, my King. You and Adviser Lauren have well stated the importance of this quest, and you will have my- our- full cooperation. But if I may, the monks I studied under only briefly referred to God's Ore and its qualities. I almost felt they avoided the subject, as if it were a dark time for mankind."

"It was, Gadlynn. A blatant display of the corruption of men.

Their lust for power eventually sealed their own doom. Lauren, I believe it time to give our esteemed First Ranger here a lesson in history. Would you be so kind?"

The adviser leaned forward eagerly. "Of course, my King. Ahhh, where to begin?"

Chapter 6

LESSONS IN HISTORY

An insightful treat, this was. Unexpected, too. A curated accounting of an arcane subject, from one of the wisest individuals in all of Alandora, Lauren Galvanster. There is a good reason why he is the King's closest adviser. Knowledgeable on most every subject, yet especially learned in the histories of our world. He was the perfect teacher, and I... I was doing my best to hide a smile. I felt like a young lad experiencing his first encounter with sweets!

Adviser Lauren began to recount the details of God's Ore: Its discovery, the revelation of its power, dark enchantments from outcast Priests, the pursuit of its possession and the ruin it would bring.

One of the many gifts God has granted me (besides humility) is that of a good memory. So, instead of dialog directly from our dear Lauren, I shall write its substance here for you now.

If I may -

To the south of Alandora, across the Darkwater Sea lays the continent of Glaase. A land similar to ours, fir trees interspersed among rolling hillsides, surrounded by white-topped mountains.

The only major differences are those of languages and gods.

From the best Lauren could determine, it had been during the reign of King Iddler, some 300 hundred years before our time, that the most important discovery of the ages was found: White Gold.

It happened at the base of Ruin Mountain, near the thriving city of Andaar. A gem mining operation, to their amazement, unearthed a large vein of this gold. They soon realized the rarity of this material, and it was not long before news spread of the discovery. Multiple parties began attempting searches, scrabbling for the promise of riches that were to come. Yet, it was all for naught. Once word reached King Iddler, he seized the entire mountainside, and those not cowed by his royal right were ruthlessly persuaded by the sword.

To add context, I must elaborate: regular gold is rare and valuable for a reason. It is possessed of a luxurious, rich sheen and pliability that allows the smith to craft and fashion ornaments with relative ease compared to that of other minerals.

White Gold, before the discovery, was simply common gold laced with metals to add further durability and strength beyond that of its original composition. The magnitude of this discovery's importance was due to this being "natural" white gold- it had never been seen before. And what was thought of as a boon of riches was only the beginning. They had yet to learn of its true uniqueness. This gold was magical!

Documentation from renowned scholar Father Ashworth reported that the Kingdom of Areth, a close ally of King Iddler, observed strange happenings among their King's sons. Areth's King Agglemore had three Princes, all of whom King Iddler had blessed with gifts of jewelry crafted from God's Ore for their loyalty to Iddler's crown.

Father Ashworth noted directly,

"King Agglemore's sons, now blessed with Gifts from King Iddler, have commented on slight euphoric feelings upon their usage of said Gifts. The baffling discovery was their new found abilities. Dalin, the oldest son, was known for being quite stout. After wearing the necklace given him, his strength nearly doubled. He often would show demonstrations of his new talent and would amaze the masses. His two younger brothers, not being born with the strength of Dalin, yet also gained increases to their natural agility. They both became expert swordsmen. With the exception of a few sword masters, the only challenge they had was against each other".

Newfound abilities came upon all who received the King's gifts... Different talents and capabilities were soon discovered and documented. Most items doubled the existing talent of the user,

meaning if you were naturally strong you would greatly increase in strength. The same had been found to apply to wisdom, agility, speed and a few other talents. Also unique was the gift of personality and charm (This conforms to our suspicions with Baron Alto). A few very rare items also increased Sorcery, or what we call Dark Magic.

I must mention that in the lands of Glaase, before the discovery of God's Ore, very little magic existed. Sure, the occasional magician would fascinate the onlookers with some staged trickery or sleight of hand, but nothing of true, unexplained magic. Yet there was a rare sect of devotees who studied this skill nonetheless. So when the discovery of this “magical” gold was revealed, every attempt was made to acquire these items for themselves, using any means necessary.

Their pursuit was highly successful. This sect soon formed an Order, calling themselves the Tardahl (in eastern Glaase meaning Dark Followers), for being faced with the choice of how to use this incredible power, they blatantly choose to walk the dark path as Sorcerers. Without the King’s knowledge, they would often hold dark rituals deep in the earth, at the source of the ore. Apparently, the goal was to increase its magical potency. Miners occasionally reported the discovery of blood applied to the walls. Animal or human, they were not able to determine.

This emerging mystery, especially the connection to sorcery, was quite troubling to the greedy King Iddler. It was obvious from our histories that he lacked some of the good qualities that our King Gerald possesses, but he knew better than to open up a doorway to the underworld. Unfortunately, this link to magic and especially dark magic- was discovered after hundreds of items had already been crafted and distributed. Poor King Iddler found himself in a conundrum and events were already unfolding faster than his ability to react.

During the fall, on a special eve, the Tardahl performed a unique ritual including a sacrifice. These writings from a high-ranking member were found in an old journal:

Tonight, sadness fills my heart, for I will miss the gathering on this appointed eve. My distant Brethren will filter into the mine's depths for a special sacrifice. If not for the importance of this specific retrieval in northern Andaar, my party and I would be in attendance. Lord Tar-gahn, God of the Underworld, be pleased and bless us with more of the precious gold.

We know with certainty that their purpose there was guided by evil intent and the end result was cataclysmic: the entire mining region was consumed in a mighty fireball! It was reported that more than 12,000 perished that horrible night. The thriving city of Andaar was no more.

The King's seat of power was spared from the brunt of this explosion thanks to thick castle walls, but not from the further sorrow and tragedy that would unfold.

Unearthly sickness and disease followed, and many died in the efforts to rebuild. The King and council declared the lands plagued, decreeing the construction of "New" Andaar many leagues to the west, near the bay of Valada. It was there that this new kingdom would remain. In the beginning, New Andaar was challenged by many adversities, yet now it is a thriving, powerful city and a jewel of commerce.

It grieves this monk's soft heart to revisit the history of

God's Ore and Old Andaar. Adviser Lauren's retelling has shed new light on this sad account. Such a needless tragedy.

What began with good intentions quickly spiraled into a pit of darkness and greed. I have always wondered...when we find unmistakable fulfillment and joy in something, why do we eventually become unsatisfied and seek to replace it with something better?

God grant me contentment.

On the subject of contentment, some might ask, "What would happen if a wealthy lord sought to acquire multiple artifacts of God's ore and wore them at the same time? They would be practically invincible!" And so we find another of the mineral's oddities: every attempt to wear more than one item at a time results in instant sickness or burning. The constant use or wearing of these items would result in various physical and mental distress and health issues. Why this is? Nobody knows.

There is only one reported case of anyone able to wear multiple artifacts at once. This happens to be in recent-day New Andaar, where the legendary High Commander Gaeleon served his king with distinction. So, impressed with Gaeleon's accomplishments and victories overseas, King Aldrin reached deep into his treasuries and honored Gaeleon's magnificent achievements with the highest of rewards: a variety of magical items. He did this even at the neglect and disagreement of his only son, Prince Dalton.

Eyewitnesses account for Gaeleon's use of an overabundance of jewelry crafted with God's Ore. Rings, necklaces, bracelets, even a stunning belt of hardened black leather laced and adorned with gems. He became Gaeleon the Gifted, a man untouched by the side effects that plagued all others. To this day he has never been defeated in single combat with or without the use of this magic. He remains the most uniquely talented and feared individual in all of Glaase.

I am truly making an assumption here, but it was probably the continued praise and adoration from King Aldrin and the kingdom that finally resulted in the downfall of Gaeleon. The envious Gaeleon decided he wanted to be King and attempted a coup. Fortunately, Prince Dalton discovered his plot and foiled his plan, but not without much bloodshed. To King Aldrin's deepest regrets, he was obligated to execute Gaeleon for his crimes against his King.

Yet King Aldrin could not find it in his heart to kill his most prestigious commander and chose to cast him out instead. Gaeleon the Fallen and all of his supporters were banished to the forsaken and plagued lands of Old Andaar. Poor King Aldrin, Gaeleon was like a son to him. It is a pity that the well-meaning king did not abide by kingdom law, because word is now that Gaeleon is raising an army, biding his time to strike back. Who knows what profane distortion now curses him and his fellow “dark-kin”?

Chapter 7

ONWARD FOR THE KING

The room was silent; not even the servants and guards were heard. A tale as sobering as this makes one reflect on one's own pursuits.

Such a shame about Gaeleon the Fallen, still residing in those God-forsaken mountains with his followers. There are rumors that the disease-plagued lands are twisting them, contorting them into beings most unnatural and grotesque--yet that sounds utterly fantastic. Most likely hearsay from unreliable sources. It will be interesting to see what transpires with time.

Hopefully peace shall remain the bedrock of New Andaar, along with its surrounding kingdoms and even those across the Darkwater sea.

King Gerald was the first to speak, breaking the contemplative silence and drawing our minds back from the reaches of historic rumination. With a temperate tone, he spoke.

"Thank you, Lauren, for that most in-depth narration on the historic matters of these artifacts of power. My most honorable guest, I am certain you now realize why we have great concern over the whereabouts and usage of these objects, and that great caution must be used in obtaining them. If all goes according to plan and the results are favorable, we shall reenlist your efforts on other God's Ore-related missions. The Kingdom has acquired multiple leads and suspicions on other locations that eventually will have to be investigated. Yet for now, this should be fairly straightforward. Brother Matthew, First Ranger Gadlynn, you have your assignment. Are there any further questions?"

Gadlynn shook her head no, possibly as dazed as I, with numerous inquiries swirling around, trying to pierce the cloudy details of the who, what, why and how of proceeding with this Kingly-declared "straight forward" quest. Somehow when the focus was on my reply, I found my mind so entwined with various questions that I was only able to meekly proclaim, "Any possibilities of having my boots re-fitted? My feet, they tend to blister easily..."

Adviser Galvanster and our good King both abruptly smiled, while Gadlynn had a look of- could it be, that of irritation? Of me? I am certain the source of this had to be something other than myself. You would never hear me complaining... much.

"Of course, Brother Matthew!" said the King, clearly enjoying the opportunity to magnanimously supply footwear.

"Boots, or any other supplies that might assist to further our cause. You need only inquire to the Quartermaster. He will ensure that you are well equipped."

"My King, was there not another matter in Greensdale to consider?" supplied Lauren.

"Ah, yes. I nearly forgot. It seems the locals there are having an issue with a pack of wolves or a renegade bear."

Gadlynn's ears perked up. She continued listening with renewed focus.

"Livestock is missing, but what is most disturbing is that a few villagers are missing as well. They have made multiple attempts to track down the beasts responsible, but have failed… Gadlynn?"

"If it is true," she considered, "and this animal or pack has developed a taste for human blood, it means they no longer fear man and most likely will attack again. I can track it down and eliminate the problem, if that is your wish."

"I have been notified," the King continued, "that they are being extra cautious and even have the nearby garrison on patrol. So, it could very well be resolved before you even arrive. Should the opportunity present itself, by all means assist, or... extinguish the menace. Yet be tactful. Villagers can be unpredictable at times; be certain to obtain permission or know this action is welcomed. We wouldn't want to be in a position of stealing some 'great' hunter's glory, now would we?"

"The village that couldn't handle their own affairs," I added. "Could be perceived negatively if we are not careful."

"Point well made. Very good, with this conference at a close, I suggest you take a few days and make preparations. The journey should be no more than two weeks' time, if all goes according to plan."

"My King," offered Gadlynn, "I am sufficiently prepared to journey at this very moment, if need be."

"You Rangers are famous for your ability to march out in an instant. This has always impressed me. Yet this task before us is not of an urgent nature, so it is safe to assume your new traveling companion could value a few days before your departure. To tie up loose ends, as they say."

"Thank you, my King," I said, perhaps with more enthusiasm than necessary. "I have many 'loose' ends."

Giving our proud First Ranger a glance, I believe I saw the slightest measure of a scowl, it certainly was not a smile. She quickly looked back to the King. He then stood, and the rest of us joined him.

"Spring is in full bloom," said Lauren, "weather should be accommodating to your journey. I most welcome your prompt return, and look forward to hearing marvelous details of your successful undertaking.

My King, is there anything else I may assist you with?"

"That shall be everything at this time, most honorable Adviser Lauren. And again, very well done on our history lesson with God's Ore."

Lauren then delivered impressive, courteous bows to each of us.

"My King, Brother Matthew, most talented First Ranger, I bid you all good day and safe travels."

After heartfelt farewells and a gracious exit from our noteworthy Adviser, the King gathered us in closer for some parting thoughts. "Before your departure, I feel it worthwhile to review some recommendations..." When our good King "recommends" a thing or two, it is best to not receive it as a mere recommendation, but as a commandment. Trouble finds the one who assumes a Kingly recommendation is malleable- trust me, I know this from experience!

"Gadlynn, you are to lead and guide the two of you safely there and back. Take care of the business at hand, and afterwards report back to me as soon as possible. Farewell to the both of you."

He sincerely bowed (most kings would never dare lower themselves in this way!) and walked out and down the hallway. A wise bit of advice, declaring the "who's in command" order of things.

Everybody knows where they stand from the beginning, no second guesses or inflated egos demanding leadership of this small entourage. Good, I can focus on keeping notes to enter into my journal upon our return. Yes, I am glad Gadlynn is taking the lead, it's the way it should be. She is, after all, First Ranger of the King!

Chapter 8

INTO THE WILDS

Two days hence, I was packed and eager to get this adventure underway... or over with, one of the two. I hadn't decided which yet. I tightly strapped food and supplies onto the mule for the two of us. I shall be overseeing the cooking and cleaning. Suits me just fine, I am a rather gifted cook and will use this skill to uncover those deep secrets and feelings Gadlynn is guarding so fervently. A full, content stomach (along with some good strong wine) has a positive way of loosening up the tongue.

Besides, I could never survive two weeks gnawing on dried venison like she is accustomed to!

My sensitive feet received a most welcomed surprise yesterday.

Along with the pack mule, Florence, came a rather gorgeous gelded black stallion handed over to me from one of the royal guards. He recited a message from our King.

"Brother Matthew, with your feet, why walk when you can ride?" the sour-faced guard recited methodically. "DO NOT tickle Bitter's ears. All the best." He handed over the reins and departed immediately without another word. Soldiers, hmph! Never time for pleasantries.

So this was an unexpected turn of events, yet was this a help or a hindrance? With a SOUR name like "Bitter" my only hope is the opposite disposition was given out of jest: instead of bitter, this fine creature was happy, joyful and incredibly fond of overweight monks. Lord, let it be!

After working with the new help, I realized that, though slightly stubborn, they were fairly receptive to my handling.

Florence, strong and stout, took the load without a single moan or complaint. Bitter was thankfully not tart or sour, nor in the mood for bucking off monks on this fine morning, for which I am grateful. So after a few waves and farewells to the neighbors that matter, we made our way out of the quaint village of Halbrin and followed north along the Swiftwash river road.

With Florence in tow and mounted on the monk-loving Bitter (Lord willing), I shall follow this road up to the village of Tarnah.

Gadlynn has a relative there and requested we gather at this location. It's efficient, being on the way, so it was of little consequence on my part.

Even though I make quite the ruckus over the delicacy of my poorly-conditioned feet, I do like traveling at times. With staff in hand, I would occasionally wander off in any certain direction, going wherever my legs would take me.

To soak in the greenery of the expansive countryside or to hear and smell the spray from the mighty Swiftwash River is refreshing to the senses- even one's soul. Most often, like today, I would venture forth in spring, with its newborn flowers and grasses, cherry trees illuminating pinks in the grandest of ways. Nature, reborn from a dormant winter, makes one appreciate the splendor and artistry involved. The countryside's spring landscape provides the setting for a Master artist to paint the most majestic of portraits. I found myself looking abroad at the visual treat and then up to the heavens and nodding my appreciation and approval. The ultimate artist. Well done, well done indeed.

Homesteads frequently dwelt along the Swiftwash, with more growing daily. Families enriched by prosperous trade along the river, and the fertile farming to the east, produced an influx of settlers ready to try their hand at this ever-growing opportunity. These families and settlers would eventually unite into a village, offering each other companionship and safety in numbers. Our continent of Alandora is riddled with villages both large and small, with periodic castles protruding from the landscape. These castles are normally owned by a Baron or Lord who answers to the King directly. They speak on behalf of the barony's needs and the needs of their subjects (at least the honorable ones do).

Allowing commoners a voice was very important to King Gerald. He sees this as just and on one occasion I overheard him arguing with a rather brash Baron. The King stated, "If God hears our voice, is it because of status or wealth? Nay, we are all equals under his eye. We just happen to be blessed with our positions of authority and because of this responsibility, this higher calling, we should make every effort to listen to their concerns and try to be fair and just in every manner possible."

I remember the King speaking with elegance and conviction, yet the baron's eyes were glazed and distant. He nodded out of courtesy, but the insight given registered into that man's head about as successfully as a woodpecker attempting to bore through a stone wall. He just could not comprehend why King Gerald did not demand more out of the common folk- demand more productivity, cooperation, taxes, and especially dedication to the Lords and Barons directly under the King. In his view only those of noble birth or status should be allowed proclamations to the throne. A King, listening to mere commoners?

Now there is wisdom.

You would not find wisdom a brief four days' travel west: There sits Grey Castle and the domain of King Falnar who, supported by his Witch Queen Lavara, rules with an iron fist. With her help, and those allies of like mind, he plots to overtake all of Alandora. He has tried strategic military maneuvers on three different occasions, yet fortunately the warriors of Ordania under King Gerald repelled his attacks. King Gerald suspects that it is just a matter of time before another attempt is made.

I often find myself praying for Falnar's reign to collapse or be overthrown from within, perhaps from someone who might possess the ability to rule with compassion and wisdom, not through brutality and fear. Yet until those prayers are answered we must remain vigilant, especially with an enemy so close.

Slightly before noon, I entered into the small village of Tarnah and was quickly joined by none other than the First Ranger herself. It went smoothly- there was no need for me to ask around the village for her whereabouts or pester some of the locals. No, she just quietly slipped out from between two barns and trotted into the lead, mounted on a rather handsome dark brown Friesian. Straight beautiful black hair draped down from one side, an impressive mount she named "Blackwing." She mentioned there was no reason to halt progress, her business was taken care of. It seems a cousin of hers was in need of some monetary help to purchase an additional cow. An expanding family has needs which a person like myself, living in solitude, does not realize. There is much responsibility in raising a family and tending a farm, seeing to all others needs before your own.

At times I miss the opportunity to be that father figure, a steadfast companion to a significant other, but when I took my vows I also agreed I would make every effort possible to be content with my decision. Besides, I have unique liberties most married men would be envious of! I can read into all hours of the night, visit anywhere at any time I choose, and drink: drink how much and whenever I feel the need (which is often, I might add.) Yes, freedoms with no one questioning or interfering are perks for those in my position! Hmmm... yet the love of a good woman and the raising of children- my own sons and daughters- is very desirable...

Ha! Listen to me... Lord help me be content!

We made good progress. Thankfully, the weather was favorable, and before the sun passed out of view, welcoming in the nighttime stars, we had reached the flourishing city of Darnell.

It was taverns and inns mostly, yet they had another reason travelers visited them, which made sure those taverns and inns stayed full. Darnell had something in their possession other river cities were envious of: The city of Darnell owned their own bridge.

Some 120 years back, Samuel Darnell- who was quite the innovator, our records show- saw that the wide, formidable Swiftwash River narrowed at this location. Where normally the river ran wide all along its course, here, at this location, it flowed deep. This allowed the natural flow to continue yet not demand as much land mass.

It was the perfect location for a bridge. So Samuel set about planning and designing how this monolithic structure could become a reality. He only mentioned his idea to a few, but once word got out on his intentions, all the naysayers and critics would not let him rest. Every opportunity for ridicule, they pounced. But Ol' Samuel believed. He believed in his vision and he believed he was the one man in all of Alandora capable enough to make it happen. I assume he almost felt like Noah and that boat of his! Have you ever read in books or scrolls about ordinary folks who

have accomplished little? No! You read about heroes, conquers and those that rise above mediocrity. These are the ones who refused to listen about what they could not accomplish and believed in what they could accomplish. They listened to their hearts, that inner voice guiding them, and did whatever it took to complete their vision or quest. The reason this bridge is aptly named the Darnell bridge is because of Samuel's ability to mute the voices of negativity and focus on what could actually be possible with ingenuity and hard work. And sitting on the bank of the Swiftwash

River one star-filled evening, a plan began to form. A structure, fashioned by river rock, that just might work.

He envisioned a two-pronged approach. In the middle of summer, when the water was at its lowest, he constructed wide and deep stone bases on both sides of the river, straight across from each other. In these foundations, he included stout metal anchors at precise locations. From these anchor points he began to fasten and stretch across multiple layers of thick hemp rope.

From there he began the more precarious tasks of building a log template to hold secure the stone masonry work until it dried and settled. Its strength came from the stone formed in a half circle, beginning low at both bases and meeting higher at the midpoint. Gravity naturally strengthened the entire structure. I marvel at such brilliance!

Soon we found more-than-adequate lodgings at an inn called the "Fancy Maid." The hostess was pleasant and the two of us soon devoured a delicious hot meal (unfortunately, with very limited conversation.) Then came our "good nights" and "sleep wells" (More I than her, trust me on this), and soon early morning was upon us. Bellies full with fried eggs and honey bread, we mounted our horses and trotted over this majestic structure of a bridge. We came into the low-lying grasslands known as the

Flowing Flats, named for the wide stretches of wheat grown and farmed for as far as the eye could see. In the summer, when the wind rolls out in strong gusts from the east, the wheat stalks flow and ripple like an ocean of gold. Enchanting. It is from here that most wheat is harvested and sold throughout Ordania.

Thinking on this makes me hungry for another serving of honey bread!

Since we were traveling in the springtime, this would-be spectacle was mostly overturned, muddied earth prepared for seeding. The only solid ground was the Eastset road on which we traveled. We followed the Eastset for half a day's ride, branching north at the village of Two-Forks and entered into the hill-land woods. This forest is at the base of Mt. Goor, and fortunately the winter was mild enough to not impede our travels. We rode at a comfortable pace, no need to rush. Nothing was urgent or of a dire need, so at nightfall we found ourselves a comfortable campsite not far from the road. By my calculations, the two of us should arrive in Greensdale by late afternoon tomorrow. My feet are so grateful for Florence and my trusted steed Bitter!

It seemed I was almost through unpacking our mule when I saw that Gadlynn already had a nice fire ablaze. This prompted me to hurry about setting up my sleeping arrangements and begin the preparation of tonight's supper. My culinary skills were demanding to be witnessed, so my plan was to create a dried venison stew of the ages when she surprisingly stated,"I've had some jerky, I'm going to retire."

"No!" My mouth opened in protest, my hands presenting the cookware. The word bellowed out of me before I had time to consider how it would sound.

"No? Are you going to force feed me, priest?" she countered.

"Not at all, Ranger, " I said, rolling the word around carefully. (Two could play at this game) "I just responded- perhaps a tad bluntly- because I was concerned you would miss out on one of the most favorable AND savorable-"

"You're making up words," she cut in.

"I'm allowed to make up words; I am a master wordsmith. And besides I've already had a few strong pulls off my wine flask, so I have every good reason to make up words!" I protested.

"Well," Gadlynn replied, "I need neither your... whatever it is you're concocting-"

"Stew... Venison stew!"

"Or your wine. I will stick with water."

I was flabbergasted. Choosing water over a fine vintage wine? It was almost heresy!

"Water? Over wine?" I gasped. "My Good Lord and I are in

agreement, he turned water into wine! Why? Because wine tastes good and helps one's motivation. Where is the flavor in water, tell me? Water is good for making mud not for combining with a savorable venison stew! Water has the consistency of... of-"

"Water" Gadlynn interjected.

"Exactly! What kind of a pleasurable experience can one take from that? Wine, at least good wine, has the substance and aroma of grapes harvested straight from the vine on a late summer's day and then meticulously transformed-"

"Do you mean squashed?"

"No! I mean transformed! Transformed into a delicate maroon liquid, then encouraged and allowed to-"

"Rot?" she supplied. With a- no, would she dare?-a smirk!

"Rot?! Nay! Age, allowed to age! AND through this methodical process called 'fermentation' does the wine get transferred into a marvelous libation unequal to all others... in my humble opinion!"

She laid down on her bedroll and propped her head up with a hand. She looked at me calmly and added,"Is this fermentation the part of the wine that is responsible for addling your wits?"

I walked over and began putting my cooking utensils away. "Yes."

More rabbit jerky for me tonight.

Chapter 9

ROADSIDE INTERRUPTIONS

I had not slept well that night- my stomach being soured by too much jerky and too much Ranger- yet we arose at sunrise and began on our way to the village. The wind picked up and tossed small branches all about, and soon the forest floor was littered with them. One unfortunate fir branch flew down and lodged itself right between Bitter's ears, lying flat on the middle of his head. He shook his head a few times to no avail, so I, his beloved master and caretaker, began a compassionate removal of poor Bitter's irritant. I grabbed the branch, twisting it so as not to scrap his ear, yet apparently not carefully enough because Bitter swiftly turned his head and BIT my left leg.

"OOWWWW!" I erupted, the echo rebounding throughout the forest.

Gadlynn stopped, turned her horse to face me.

"What did you do to him?" she asked. "(Do to him? Do to him? !)"

"I simply removed a branch stuck on his head! When I plucked it away, he bit me!" I replied angrily.

Now, I am opposed to the mistreatment of animals of any

kind they being God's creation and all- yet at this very moment I must confess, the thought of a retaliatory blow of some sort did cross my mind. Yet I held my leg, groaned in pain, and promptly remembered the instructions the King gave: DO NOT tickle his ears! I certainly will not be doing any "tickling" of his ears. As a matter of fact, if there is any tickling to be done, it will be by me with a large tree branch swiftly leveled against his... I caught myself. Then muttered, "Lord help me learn my lessons without anger and wear my bruises proudly."

Gadlynn heard this and offered, "Why would you get angry at him? Bitter has served you well. You probably did something to irritate him."

She said it in such a way it was clear that in her mind it had eliminated any debate. Yet that did not settle well with me.

"Irritate him?" I questioned incredulously. "If removing an obstruction from on top of his head justifies him BITING me then maybe it is I who have the right to be... irritated." My reply seemed rather logical to me.

"Maybe you should try riding Florence instead."

As she trotted away, I loudly offered, "Perhaps I will request metal leg guards from the King next time!"

I gingerly guarded my thigh and spurred Bitter on. I looked back, smiled at Florence. She was content tagging along from her leash which was tied to my saddle. If I had to hold her reins the entire journey, I do believe my arm would eventually fall off. "We shan't have that now, shall we?"

The two of us traveled on through the Hilland woods without many interruptions, only passing one trade wagon in the process. The road began to ascend aggressively as we came closer to the Mt. Goor pass.

Not a road actually traversing up and over the summit of the mountain, just midway, about the highest elevation travelers and wagons could handle without becoming too steep or treacherous. Once over the pass we shall be roughly half a day's journey to Greensdale. Unfortunately, at this rate the last leg of the journey very well could happen in the dark. It is hard to determine exactly when you will arrive when traveling horseback or walking, for that matter. Eventually the road peaked and we began our descent. Our rides certainly appreciated the difference in grade. Not too much further on, we entered into a dense section of forest when Gadlynn suddenly held up her fist.

It was done in such a way that demanded I immediately halt and shut myself up.

She was gazing deep into the woods up the mountainside to our left. On this cloudy day, crowded fir trees laced with moss and ivy filtered out the majority of the sun. Ferns and vine maples, along with occasional broken rocks, blanketed the ground. The combination of all of this made it visually limited. Yet she was seeing something...or sensing something. I saw her nose move slightly; I do believe she was smelling the air. Hopefully, for her nose's sake, the horses did not choose this exact moment to... ummm, allow any "build up" to exit their bodies.

Here, at this possibly precarious moment and this is what I was thinking? I almost laughed out loud. Like a small child in church, in the still silence of the service, attempting to stifle themselves from bellowing out laughter for no other reason than you are not supposed to bellow out laughter at this time. It seems the more you're not supposed to do something, the more apt you are to do it! Funny thing our human nature.

And so, like one lacking a good measure of wits, I let out a small chuckle.

"SHHHH" she warned, silencing me. Gadlynn slowly dismounted and motioned that I do the same. Heeding her instruction, I slowly slid off Bitter and approached her.

"What is it?" I whispered.

She looked me in the eyes. I easily gathered she was concerned.

"There is something in that direction, in those thickets, something... disturbing."

I looked, saw nothing. "Disturbing? As in bandits or Falnar's men?"

"No. Not human, a beast of some sorts," she explained.

"How are you certain? I can see nothing in there" I asked, implying for a more detailed explanation.

"I just know. I know the scent of humans and those of animals, and this animal... my intuition tells me, is highly dangerous…and that is why... I'm going to investigate."

My inner voice had a hard time comprehending 'highly dangerous' and 'going to investigate'. I found this course of action illogical and only the worst result would be the outcome. I attached my most prudent and caring 'wisdom' face and pleaded, "Is the risk worth investigating? What if something truly monstrous is out there and something happens to you? The King would blame me, I know he will!"

"Shhhh..." She quieted down my lack of investigative enthusiasm and continued, "I'm not concerned about my welfare or yours, to a certain degree. I am concerned about a family's wagon passing by at the wrong time when that thing is hungry or in a foul mood."

Compassion won. I responded, "Pardon my fear- fear of the unknown and fear for your safety... but you have the right of it. I will tie up the horses and grab my staff."

"You will do NO such thing," she whispered insistently. "You will stay here and have the horses ready to ride at an instant. You will wait upon my return."

"I can be an able backup to you. I am quite good with my staff," I pleaded. I recognized that if she was willing to face this dangerous whatever it is, I should be willing to accompany her. It is only right. We are partners on this venture, she being the leader of course, yet here we are: comrades. I like that. We are comrades. Despite the fact that she is very stone-headed.

"No. You would only slow me down. Besides the King would blame me if anything were to happen to you!"

I began to object, but she gestured for me to shut it.

"Not another word. Remember, I'm in charge. Have the horses ready."

With that, she unlatched her cloak, fastened it to her saddle bag, took her bow from its sheath, and disappeared into that dreaded, dire section of forest.

I wondered, what on earth could be out there? Black bear, mountain lion... dragon? Dragon! But they don't exist anymore or are not supposed to- that's what history tells us. "Let the histories ring true," like our good King says. Yes, let there be no more dragons!

While waiting for her return, I slid down and watered up

our fine steeds. Afterward I found myself quietly speaking a couple of thoughtful prayers on her behalf. I asked our good Lord to guide her safely and grant her protection, as any concerned comrade would do. It is possible, I also could have mentioned asking for some kind of passageway through that thick rock that sits on her shoulders... when a thunderous CRASH shook me out of my thoughts. This crashing was followed by more crashing and the sounds of small trees breaking. I instantly mounted Bitter, readied Florence and steadied Gadlynn's beloved Blackwing. I fearfully looked toward the hillside, dreading what could possibly be the source of this, yet I could see nothing...

nothing except-

The thicket in the distance parted as if there was a massive boulder crashing through the underbrush, rolling over whatever happened to lie in its path. The horses grew skittish, and I calmed them as best I could. I kept looking.

"Gadlynn!" I cried out. If she were to trip during her escape, this humongous rock would crush her in an instant. The sounds grew nearer, louder, until finally I was able to see the boulder.

Except it wasn't a boulder, it was the most massive mountain bear I have ever seen!

At a blazing speed, it bowled everything over in its path.

Gadlynn, at a full run, sprung out of the underbrush near me, screaming, "GOOOO!"

As I held Blackwing steady, Gadlynn leaped forward as if having wings, landing on top of her steed, and our party of five began the most horrifying escape I have ever taken part in.

First off, if not for the denseness of this forest, ol' brown fur would have been supping on Ranger and one tasty monk. Maybe just monk... Gadlynn would elude the creature somehow, being "gifted" the way she is. So that being mentioned, the instant we darted off, that bear was in high pursuit. Wind whipped in our faces, our ears overwhelmed by the deafening roar of the horses' hooves slamming down on the roadway. I was concerned for Florence; I should have unpacked her!

Surprisingly, for a pack mule fully loaded, she ran far better than expected. It is impressive what kind of athletic results can be achieved when being chased by an extraordinarily massive, angry bear. Still, as noble an effort Florence was giving, that monster was gaining, and in mere moments the thing would have her.

A whizzing sound flew past my left ear. Gadlynn had formed alongside me and was launching arrows at the beast. It was quite the sight to behold, her navigating all this while riding at a full run. How could she keep her balance, control Blackwing, twist around, notch, and deliver her attack so effectively?

Fascinating.

The panting of the horses, the lack of air filling my lungs, and that monstrosity nearly upon us, appropriately filled me with dread: I feared that we could not hold this pace much longer. I gathered my resolve and gave a quick look back.

It was horrific.

The beast was so large, it took up most of the roadway. Layers of thick matted brown fur covered its gigantic body. I then saw its eyes. Raw, black, angry eyes filled with wrath, its only desire was to rip us limb from limb. It roared out defiance, making my resolve retreat and absolute terror overrun my soul.

Its mouth gaped wide, baring fangs the size of my fingers, drool and spittle oozing out. I yelled at Bitter, spurring him on. It is time to prove your worth, horse, or we shall all perish together. I then chanced a second look.

The arrows Gadlynn had been launching were not achieving the desired effect. A few shafts were protruding out from its chest, yet it did not slow...

It just kept coming.

Kept coming like a river dam breaking apart, water bursting through, unstoppable. So this is how I shall end, I thought. How we will end. It was both quicker and stronger than anything we could contest with. The beast seems oblivious to Gadlynn's arrows... then the unthinkable- God forbid! Do I release Florence's reigns to save us? Do I? I must if we are to survive... forgive me Lord... forgive me Florence...

The bear roared in agony and stopped.

I glanced back. An arrow was sticking out of his mouth. I saw it struggle, eventually ripping it out with its paws.

It roared one last warning, a warning to never return or the unthinkable will occur, our complete annihilation. I strained my neck, looking back one more time and thank the good Lord, I saw it retreat back to whatever hell hole it crawled out of.

Relief washed over me-

Thank you, Lord, for Your mercy.

We kept a solid pace for a good long while. The mere thought of that beast renewing its resolve and pursuing again kept us focused on creating distance. Yet not willing to chance one of the horses stumbling, we eventually slowed them down to a canter. All of us worked on recovering our wind, and Gadlynn quickly decided, despite overwhelming exhaustion, it was best to travel through the night into Greensdale.

Later, we passed over a small bridge with a calm creek flowing underneath. It was here she ordered us to stop, let the horses drink, and dismount for a short time.

"We must hurry. Bears are nocturnal. If it decides to resume tracking us..." Her voice trailed off. I eagerly nodded agreement.

The night had completely descended, and the stars were shining in full spectacle in between tree branches. We were able to see along the road well enough, yet looking into the thick of the woods, nothing but complete and utter darkness. I could hear the horses drinking eagerly, probably wondering if it might be their last. I moved close to Gadlynn and quietly asked, "Gadlynn, what happened up there? What provoked it to attack?"

She sighed, glanced at the horses then to me.

"Perhaps you are aware that, for some odd reason, I have a heightened sense of smell and intuition."

"Along with other gifts, I am told," I interjected.

"Correct. Where we stopped, it was overwhelming. My thoughts told me something this intense had to be explored. Even if possibly perilous."

"At times you have to follow that inner voice," I added.

"I agree. I wove my way through the thickets for a stretch, and the scent of death... and something else... was getting stronger. I came upon a ravine lined with large boulders up and down its walls. In the center it was dark, looked to be a cave entrance. I needed a better view and crept closer, in my mind, recalling what the King mentioned about that beast the villagers are looking for"

"Yes, as long as you were that close, it made sense to see," I offered.

"Right. I was able to recognize bones and tattered cloth near the entrance. Most animals have very keen smell, far superior to mine, so I was cautious, not knowing what lay in there. Then, like thunder it ran out! I barely escaped. If not for trees and brush impeding its path... I'm not sure I..."

"You would have escaped. And you did. Living and breathing, ready for another day," I reassured.

She looked distant, somewhere else in her mind, then nodded her head in agreement. “Living and breathing...yes. Ready for another day...we need to move.”

I responded without hesitation, “I’ll gather the horses.”

Chapter 10

TALES FROM GREENSDALE

Morning's rays of sunlight sliced through thick layers of fog as the tops of dwellings began to slowly appear. As we drew closer, these structures materialized into blacksmith shops, taverns, inns and other buildings accompanying a growing and prosperous village. Only now did we hear the trumpet of the local roosters demanding that all others awaken now, simply for the reason that they were.

Prior to this, while the sun was still too bashful to show herself, we had trotted past multiple farms. Great plats of land dedicated mostly to the growing of corn, their fields freshly plowed in preparation for late-spring seeding.

The farmsteads had their family lodgings, and close to these were barns of all shapes and sizes. Mainly for storing hay and keeping their animals dry, these barns were a tempting sight for five exhausted adventures. More than once we considered acquiring "hayloft" accommodations in one of these capable structures; at this point we were not selective in the slightest.

Yet Gadlynn thought it best not to startle the good people

sleeping soundly or anger an early-morning farmer finding two strangers in his loft and three mounts taking up space, eating his hay. So we somehow found the strength within to persevere all the way into Greensdale.

After locating the nearest inn, fittingly named "The Weary Woodsman," we saw to our horses' needs and then off to the rooms we rented, to promptly collapse into unconsciousness until late afternoon.

Yet my slumber was filled with nightmares.

Most often my sleep is sound, restful. Yet that night- or rather that morning- I was plagued with dreams.

Dark, wicked dreams, the kind that, when I awoke, I was trembling and remembered vivid details. I kept recycling the chase; the bear with its brown, bulky frame and massive, open jaws pursuing me, closer and closer until finally its great paw swipes me and Bitter off the ground to be its unwilling victims.

In other dreams, it was other beasts, with the same result. One a large white wolf, one a dragon, and the most disturbing: right before I awoke, I was running from... myself.

A horrible, dark side of me, running with incredible speed, chasing, striking and pulling at my robes, demanding nothing but my complete and ultimate failure in every aspect of my existence. I would spur Bitter on and on, but it, no 'I' kept coming. It refused to be outmatched. I recall gathering as much courage as heavenly possible and looking back, seeing my face. It had a wicked smile and laughed out of spite, then mocked me, “Why bother running? I can do this all night! Your life, your efforts, are worthless.

Might as well quit! You have disgraced yourself enough, what difference are you making? No difference! You should quit and go back!”

That’s when a knock on the door awoke me. It was Gadlynn. “Come out to the hall when you’re ready.”

“I’ll be right out,” I replied.

I heard the sounds of her leaving and positioned myself on the side of the bed. I was startled to find perspiration on my brow, on this chilly spring afternoon. That was evidence to me of how intense my dreams were, especially the last. Fighting with our own selves, literally.

How many times do we talk ourselves out of pursuing lofty dreams or worthwhile goals, just by the barrage of negativity echoing from our inner voice? Who controls this voice? Common sense, reason? Or perhaps in these cases it’s fear and anxiety. I then made a resolution with myself: when I recognize negativity attempting to sway my direction, I shall do my best to wall it off. I was never a stone mason, yet, due to my tendency for the negative, I shall be doing much wall building in the near future! Help me build strong walls, Lord.

That entangled mass of dark dreams reminded me of how thankful I was to wake, feel secure, and see the room- walls around me- and know that my day was ready to begin. I soon exited my room and met Gadlynn in the dining hall sitting in the corner, surrounded by a full table of breakfast plates. The growl in my stomach told me that my timing was perfect.

"Good morning" I said cheerfully, buoyed by the sight of food.

She met my eyes and only said, "How did you sleep?" I instantly thought she might have struggled in her dreams also.

"I slept soundly... for a while, then..."

"Nightmares," she finished.

"Yes. Nightmares. What happened yesterday..."

"Was the closest to death you've ever been," the Ranger stated.

"Are you going to eat all those?"

I noticed the eggs and honey bread on the table.

With a sweep of her hand she motioned my permission to partake, and partake I did. I was famished. After annihilating three eggs in record time, I broke the silence. "Do you have a plan on how we are to approach Baron Arlo?"

"We will ask for an audience with him when he is

available. You and I will go to his Hall after we're through here," she stated.

I balanced an egg on top of my slice of bread and happily bit down, releasing yoke all about the bread *and* my beard.

She rolled her eyes up but I didn't care, it was delicious.

"Have you given any thoughts on how we are to ask him, implore him... ahhh. How we are to acquire the item?" I probed.

"I do hate speaking in situations like these," she admitted.

(What? Something she does not excel at? Maybe I'm being too harsh. No. No I'm not.) I smiled.

"I could assist you in this, if you wish?" I offered.

Her eyes shifted from mine to the hall entrance, just as two armed guards walked in, coming directly toward us. One of the guards stated, "Our most noble Lord, Baron Arlo, requests your attendance at his lodge immediately. We shall escort you."

Immediately? Might I please wash my face of egg yolk first? I thought. A bit obstinate for two guests- ambassadors from the King himself!

"Will we need our horses?" Gadlynn asked.

"No. It is within walking distance," the guard responded.

As we followed them out, I left two silver pieces for the lodgings and breakfast and leaned in close to Gadlynn, "No time like the present, hmmm?"

Her only response was motioning to clean yoke off of my chin. I did so humbly.

We were escorted across the village toward the north end, where I could see a large lodge waiting. We passed by multiple villagers adorned in their tunics and work clothes, busily making the way to wherever they were off to. The women wore simple patterned dresses with matching hair pieces, most commonly in light blues or greens. Most passersby glanced our way suspiciously. The two guards were responsible for that, walking us to our destination as if we were prisoners. Perhaps we were and we just didn't know it yet?

Gadlynn looked across the way and met the eye of a young woman leaning back against the wall of a leather shop. She wore an outfit similar to those of our Rangers. She held a bow in one hand and ate an apple out of the other. Whoever this was clearly had an interest in us maybe more in Gadlynn- but her eyes followed our every move, and once we arrived at the Baron's Hall, she threw her apple aside and made her way there too.

The guards escorted us into the foyer, which held an impressively high ceiling erected with sturdy, thick wood beams and large curved doors with massive black hinges.

Villagers made good use of these doors, smiles upon their faces, walking in and out, yet there we stood. I glanced around, taking in the architecture, when finally an advisor of sorts opened the hall door and beckoned the guards to bring us in.

We entered an elaborate, grandiose hall constructed out of wood, yet fashioned in a way where the impression was instant and lasting. It was some of the finest wood sculpting I had ever seen. Multiple layers, mixed with different wood tones, all unique, working together as one to complete remarkable wall portraits and displays. I wonder if King Gerald has visited this Hall? Most likely he has, Greensdale being in his Kingdom and all.

A tall, charming man dressed in nobility stood talking with some commoners near an elevated wood throne, itself another fine example of craftsmanship. This indeed was our one and only Baron Arlo, the entire reason for our journey.

He noticed us and motioned us forward. I could hear villagers around me commenting on how fortunate they were to have Baron Arlo looking after their needs. A few others mentioned how handsome he was and wondered if he had ever served in battle when he was younger. Then I spotted her again- the girl who watched us like a hawk out in the street. She positioned herself within ear range, for some reason extremely motivated to hear our conversation. I glanced over at Gadlynn. Her demeanor, always confident and self-assured, now looked stiff and apprehensive. I tried to get her attention so I could give her some assurance, yet she stared straight ahead at the Baron and took a knee when we were close. Not trying to make her feel out of place or lack any "Barony" etiquette, I joined her, one knee on the floor, head lowered.

Baron Arlo politely asked his entourage if their conversation could continue at another time. They smothered him with high praise and reactions of how "Blessed" they were to have his attention for as long as they had, him being Lord over Greensdale and all. I thought their comments were rather over-affectionate, yet I should not be too judgmental. It was most likely well deserved. He had an aura about him that was quite agreeable-pleasing in fact. It made me grateful that he would see Gadlynn and I so soon upon arriving.

I shook away my thoughtful first impressions of the good Baron Arlo as he spoke out for all to hear,"Good people of Greensdale, please hear me now. We are truly blessed to have representatives from none other than our beloved King Gerald with us here today!"

This was greeted by some hand clapping and positive "Ooohs!" (It's nice to be loved by the people, isn't it?) He continued, "Please, stand and be seen..."

He gestured with his hand in a wide, fluid motion, capturing the attention of the entire room with his theatrical display. We promptly stood and found ourselves smoothing our outfits. Even I, in my plain brown robe, was very motivated to make a grand impression to the Baron.

He continued to speak, "You have graced us today, venturing all this distance to bless our remote Kingdom of Greensdale (Did he just say 'Kingdom?') certainly to bring us tidings and assurances of continued peace with King Falnar? What do King Gerald's humble Brother Matthew and his "legendary" (He said that in a way almost in mock, Gadlynn did not seem to notice) First Ranger need to share with the good people of Greensdale on this grand occasion?"

With the mention of the First Ranger, the girl from out in the street exclaimed rather loudly, "I knew it!" refocusing the entire room onto her. She retreated from her mild outburst while the Baron looked her way, frowning slightly, which instantly produced, "Forgive me, my Lord…"

"Of course! A realistic response from having prominent servants of the King in our midst," he said, comforting her, and with the entire room at his command he continued, "Pardon the interruption. So, what was the news that you wished to share? Hopefully a new proclamation from the King of reduced taxes for all in his Kingdom!" That was followed by laughter because they all knew that wasn't going to happen. A clever one, this Baron

Arlo.

Gadlynn responded, "Baron Arlo and all good people of Greensdale, we are here on behalf of the King to... request permission to consult privately with the Baron on matters of the King's concern."

I thought that was well-delivered, despite the unusual pressure of being the focus of the entire Hall. The Baron brushed her request aside, saying, "A private audience? 'Miss' First Ranger, I pride myself in being open with the people of my province, both of low birth and of high. Whatever it is that you need to ask or share, undoubtedly can and will be presented to all of us."

With that statement I heard various complements, agreements and some whispers of "there is wisdom".

Gadlynn responded, "I would respectfully ask you to reconsider. The subject matter is private and concerns you alone."

Yet, for some reason he was resistant to this suggestion. Baron Arlo came across as an honest, upright, wise leader; it aroused in me a slight suspicion of why he would refuse this mild request. Did he suspect our arrival might include inquiry into his overwhelming popularity, perhaps magically enhanced?

He responded adamantly, "Whatever it is you would say, say it openly. Unless this has to do with strategic maneuvers against Falnar's Grey Castle, which I am positive it is not, speak plainly for one and all to hear."

"Yes!" some in the audience added, along with, "That is only fair," and "The Baron is right, no need for secrecy." I immediately became aware that our discussion was going to end negatively so I found it within me to intercede. I politely spoke up, "Gadlynn, if I may?"

She turned to me and, with a small measure of relief, said, "Certainly."

I nodded to her, inwardly asked the good Lord to help guide my speech, turned my focus to the Baron and began, "Our most noble Baron Arlo and the good people of Greensdale, thank you for allowing us this opportunity to proclaim, from the King himself, our gratitude for many years of partnership in defense of our Kingdom and prosperous trade throughout the entirety of free Alandora. We are true allies!"

The crowd responded favorably, along with a few hand claps.

"As it should be, I would have it no other way," the Baron added.

I continued, "As the King's First Ranger and I were waiting in the foyer, I could not help but marvel at the architectural wonder that had been assembled here. Greensdale possesses one of the most impressive village Halls I have ever had the pleasure of observing. The design and craftsmanship involved must have been extensive, yet the end results are nothing short of extraordinary!"

"We pride ourselves in the talent of our craftsmen," said the Baron. "They are artists with wood instead of paint and canvas. The best in all of Alandora!"

I heard agreement, clapping and "Well stated," from the people around me. I continued, "The throne upon which you sit must have taken years to carve, the detail displayed... magnificent! A marvel in any village or... in any castle!" More clapping and comments of agreement. The Baron, rather pleased with the praise and proper due awarded his "Kingdom," glowed with pride at my accolades.

"Besides wood, there are other fine examples of craftsmanship in our midst today: those exquisite rings adorning your fingers. Every piece, a marvel. The necklace around your neck... expectational, without compare. Almost historical..."

His hand immediately went to hold his necklace. The rumors were true- I could see the similarities to other enchanted jewelry. Its detail, construction... its sheen. Just then I noticed a slight bluish ripple pulsate from the intricate white gold laced throughout the strands. God's Ore, without a doubt.

"It is quite a rare piece," the Baron supplied quickly, "a recent gift from my beloved wife. An old heirloom on her father's side."

"And with all due respect and high regard, this heirloom is why we are here today. As representatives of the King, the First Ranger and I sought a more private conversation. Yet since you insisted on 'openness', we must state our King's desire plainly... we want to purchase the necklace."

The room was silent. Baron Arlo looked down, paced a few steps, looked me directly in the eye and stated, "Absolutely not." I suspected difficulty from the outset, but this might prove to be more challenging than walking through a castle wall- castle wall, hmmm...?

"The King has supplied us with a fair sum of gold and jewels in exchange" I offered.

"Gold and jewels? If it was wealth I desired, I could barter with any noble. It has more value to me than mere coin," the Baron declared.

The Baron was very persuasive. That inner voice, beckoning me to see this his way, to relent to his will, his every wish...

Yet, I could not. I steeled my resolve and continued on, "You are aware of its uniqueness are you not?" I tactfully returned. I was doing my best to downplay the importance of the necklace, and I certainly did not want to make its abilities public knowledge.

I glanced over at Gadlynn. She looked stoic, clasping her hands behind her back as if at attention. What troubled me was the way she looked up at the Baron, almost in adoration. I must be mistaken, she adores no one except our King.

"Yes, yes, I know of its rarity, its historical value. Does King Gerald presume he can just march in here and snatch away a sacred family relic?!" the Baron protested.

The crowd was getting restless, almost defensive of their Baron.

I was becoming irritated with his attitude about the King so I replied bluntly, "He could if he so desired. He is our KING.

Yet, he is an intelligent and benevolent man and would rather acquire it by more accommodating means rather than through force. He fears the chance of your necklace falling into Falnar's hands."

"Falnar would find no easy acquisitions here. My soldiers are more than capable!" he shouted.

"They are capable... and would be better able to defend your barony and its people with a... castle," I offered, attempting to soothe his rising anger.

The crowd's mood shifted positive. I felt one of my key goals to a winning strategy was to not only convince the Baron, but to also win the room.

The Baron settled and thought out loud, “A castle... hmmm.” “With the King’s authorization and help with its designing and construction,” I added.

Gadlynn looked at me curiously, “Castle?”

I nodded. The King doesn’t know this yet, but it would be a brilliant strategic move. He has always wanted border baronies and villages to prepare their defenses more adequately. Building a castle here would be a bold, yet wise, step. King Gerald would welcome such an expenditure. I hope.

He contemplated while pacing back and forth on the platform. He stood above everyone, hand to mouth, thinking. His hand again reached and grasped the necklace. His countenance suddenly changed, his look of willingness and possibility transitioned into a confrontational mask. He looked absolute, defiant.

“No. It is mine,” stated Baron Arlo.

“It belongs to our Baron!” someone in the crowd hollered. That was followed by more verbal support for Baron Arlo.

It is settled then, I thought. The King will be forced to take more drastic measures and risk losing a crucial ally along our tenuous border. I do hope that I am not involved. To forcefully remove the necklace from this well-meaning, radiant example of leadership would be horrific.

Gadlynn suddenly spoke up, "Baron Arlo, this transaction would be highly beneficial to you and your people. To sacrifice all this potential for one mere necklace?"

"A mere necklace? You surely know it is more than that. I can not give it up and I will not hand it over. I am sorry," the Baron stated directly.

I watched as his eyes suddenly shifted to the rear of the Hall.

Shouting came from the foyer, and a villager burst in. His clothes were ragged and tear-streaked lines ran through the dirt on his face.

The villager shouted out, "My Lord! I demand to be heard."

The Baron focused on him and offered, "What is it that troubles you? Guards, bring him forward."

Two guards escorted him to the front. Gadlynn and I stepped back, making room in the center of the aisle. Upon arriving, the villager dropped to his knees and wept.

"Control yourself and share your burden; you are among friends," Baron Arlo stated compassionately. I am absolutely convinced the good Baron Arlo is truly sincere and seeks only the best for his people. He looked radiant as he reached down and took the troubled soul's hand.

"It's my Lucy... my Lucy... she is missing!" He barely got

the words out.

The girl from the street stepped forward and said, "How do you know she is missing? Were there tracks?"

The older man replied between sobs, "I... found her... dolly..." The crowd moaned and grew restless. The poor man's shaking hands held up his daughter's bloody, tattered doll--what used to be a doll. A few women shrieked.

"I... didn't see any tracks..." he continued.

The Baron lowered his head and stood. He slowly proceeded back to the platform, as if in deep mourning, bearing his brother's burden as if it were his own. I reached down to console this devastated soul. How brokenhearted and utterly lost he must feel. He clung to my arm and sobbed upon my sleeve.

The room reeled. Fear seemed to overtake all in attendance; all were affected by the recent atrocities afflicted upon their village by this hellspawn.

The Ranger-looking girl appeared frightened for but a moment, yet this fear quickly transitioned into resolve, and she shouted above the clamor, "Baron Arlo, I implore you! Please resume the hunt and track this beast down, once and for all!"

The Baron looked perplexed. His hand began to shake, he looked at her and pleaded, "We... have tried... multiple times! This 'thing'... is not natural. I am not sure...what more can be accomplished."

The crowd continued to stir. It seemed they were not receptive to the Baron's timidity. The girl from the street certainly wasn't.

"We have to do something! How many more will die from this creature?" she cried out.

This new focus on an old problem caught the Baron off guard. He appeared regal and handsome, yet this new revelation made his response come across weak and ineffective. He seemed confused and kept staring down, then up, then down.

"Yes. Yes of course... we shall send out hunting parties.

Although all other attempts have failed, we must try... yes, at the very least we must try..." His voice grew weaker as he trailed off, his tone signaling defeat.

As Baron Arlo struggled maintaining his confidence and poise in front of his people, they, in turn, grew louder in their complaints, uncharacteristically defiant to his leadership...

"QUIET!!!" Gadlynn screamed, cutting through the entire room and ushering in an instant silence.

She turned and faced the people, her entire being demanding their attention.

"I am the King's First Ranger! And I shall track down and kill this beast!! For the honor of King Gerald and for the honor and safety of Greensdale!" She stood there, alone, for all the crowd to see, and to judge.

Her gaze moved from one face to the next, staring into their eyes, and in a moment's time sharing with them much-needed compassion- compassion of the horror and frustration they were feeling in the absolute futility of their past attempts. They were stunned at the power and confidence she had just displayed.

In mere seconds she had constructed the villagers of Greensdale into a fierce ally, comrades in this renewed cause. And as the crowd slowly began to cheer, their confidence rose along with akin to a slow burning fire- the declaration of this warrior, this First Ranger, they stoked this blaze into a furnace and the crowd roared on... unstoppable!

I stood there in awe. The people shouted for vengeance, justified in their anger, seeking a final solution: conquest over this beast who has terrorized them for years. I sympathized with their resolve, yet found myself puzzled by Gadlynn. Where was this determination earlier? Was it somehow stifled by circumstances? By outside influence?

By... outside influence... hmmm, makes one ponder. Perhaps this sudden flurry of events is what it took to break free that inner fire within her? Part of my "plan" has just been accomplished by none other than the First Ranger herself.

"Win over the crowd..." No easy task, that one, yet now it is done and hopefully it will sway the Baron to capitulate to our desires, our mission.

"What is it, that you need? Your demand... to bring back its head? The Baron pleaded.

The audience quieted. All eyes looked toward the King's Ranger for a response. Gadlynn calmly shifted her connection from the people to the Baron and simply replied, "I deliver its head, you hand over the necklace."

The Baron shifted around and added, "For the gold... and for the construction of the-"

"The assistance in the design and construction of the castle," I found myself abruptly interjecting, feeling a tad awkward with the outburst and the sudden attention. "And I must add, this is strictly at the King's discretion..."

The Baron stood back, giving it some thought. Finally satisfied, he continued with a new, emboldened passion, exclaiming, "You!" He pointed directly at Gadlynn. "Deliver me, and my people, the head of this Hellspawn... and I shall honor our agreement, necklace and all, and welcome the new construction of..."

He paused, breathed in the aspirations of his fellow comrades and exalted," Castle Arlo!"

Everybody seemed to be greatly inspired because the whole hall suddenly burst into deafening cheer.

I stood there looking about, admiring everyone in the room, standing, celebrating, thinking the nightmare that has horrified them for winters upon winters will finally be put to an end.

Then amongst the cheers I saw her, the crowd's praise encouraging, yet she did her best to deflect the attention. This was not by her choice, she wanted none of this. It was not her desire, nor her way of thinking. She stood tall and shouted, "I will succeed in this. There is no room for failure! Until I return, I wish you all... farewell."

I calmly fell in behind her as she abruptly exited the hall. She was like a knight riding off to battle, the people around her cheering and clapping, smothering her with compliments. She was entirely focused and seemed completely determined of mind: the inevitable outcome, the only outcome would be that of victory.

It was shortly after exiting the building that a dread thoroughly washed over my entire being- mind, body and soul. I followed her back to the inn and noticed my hand beginning to shake, my mind becoming hard to focus. Words became so burdensome, my tongue would not let them escape my mouth. She sat back down, the same table as before, and motioned to the innkeeper she was ready to order more food. I stood near her, my head feeling faint. She stared up at me and motioned for me to sit, yet I found myself unresponsive, numb.

The realization of what lie ahead had just successfully rooted itself into my consciousness to the point of ridding away any attempt at perspective and positive conclusions. We were soon to journey back, back to that beast's lair! To return and attempt to kill something about as close to indestructible as has ever roamed the earth. Back to discuss with Death if he would kindly be willing to bypass my appointment for another time... I doubt he will agree.

We were returning to look into the eyes of hell itself and somehow make it back out alive...

I collapsed into my chair, covered my face with my hands and trembled uncontrollably...

God take this burden from me.

Chapter 11

PLANNING AND DEVELOPMENT

The task before us was certainly perilous, but you would not be able to tell by watching Gadlynn. She ordered an entire roast chicken, slices of cheese, a variety of mixed vegetables in a "Weary Woodsman Inn" special sauce, a loaf of honey bread and a few apple tarts to top it off.

Apparently, speaking to the Baron and the villagers of Greensdale was daunting work. Yet, I had no appetite, possibly the first time in my life. As she devoured the food before her, I slowly began to regain my composure, my tongue once again able to form words. Hopefully I would be advancing to complete sentences before too long.

"Last... last meal?" I stumbled out.

She tore another bite off the wing she held, followed it with a slice of cheese, swallowed and replied matter-of-factly, "Not if I have my way about it."

"Gadlynn. You don't have to do this. We can return to the King and acquire more Rangers or something, anything to even the field," I pleaded.

"We will do no such thing. The King sent us here to fulfill a mission; anything less than that is unacceptable," she stated, clearly resolute in her purpose. When this First Ranger sets her focus on something, she doesn't waver, I'll give her that. I sat back and continued to watch her eat, contemplating the circumstance before us, and finally concluded the inner battle that waged in my mind: I will cast aside all self doubt and assist her in any way possible. If I drink tea with Death and he decides to take me to the afterlife prior to my plan, then so be it. I will be reacquainted with my parents and brother and walk the heavens with my Lord; if this be my plight, let it be said, my effort was worthwhile.

Her stomach seemed to have no boundaries, so as she consumed all that which lay before her, I continued to watch, pondering. The young woman's features displayed a fierce determination that must have been pivotal in her sudden rise to prominence. How admirable, I thought, and it inspired me. I must match this resolve of hers and be willing to walk through fire in order to come through this alive. So Death be damned, I will see this through!

I broke through her focus and offered, "We should develop a plan. Detail every possible weakness and every possible advantage."

She put down her fork, which held a massive portion of that

vegetable "surprise", reminding me of a farmer pitching hay with his pitchfork and responded, "I do have a plan. My plan is to kill it."

I said in return of the obvious, "Of course... you do... what I mean is, we should rehearse every possible outcome, try to take advantage of any vulnerabilities this beast might have. You shot it at close range, it did not even penetrate its hide! Those arrows you launched would have killed any soldier... yet, the only shot that seemed to do any damage was when you got lucky and hit it in the mouth-"

I paused, realizing the indignant stare she was giving.

"Lucky? You assume my arrow hitting its mouth, luck?"

"Of course I thought it luck! Its mouth was closed during the chase, except when it roared..." I pleaded.

"The arrow landed exactly where I intended it to. It is called timing and accuracy," she fumed. I felt similar to a child during schooling, simply disciplined for a lack of understanding. I was not entirely at fault, how was I supposed to know her skill level? To make that shot... on horseback?

"Very well. I stand corrected," I conceded, then continued, "Gadlynn, all I am attempting to accomplish here is some kind of strategy, a rehearsed plan or design to aid us when we try and kill this thing."

Her eyes shifted to the side of the room and then back to mine.

"I will give you this, a well thought out plan, especially in a case like this, is crucial. One thing is a fact, that monster's hide is incredibly thick. We need to develop... something, maybe a new weapon... one that can penetrate. That can deliver a 'kill' shot."

My hand went to my face as I pondered. The cogs in my mind where beginning to turn... beginning to construct... to devise an idea. A method of delivery that could send this creature into the abyss- if there is such a place for creatures, of that I know not.

"And by the way, except for the planning part, there is no we," she stated, interrupting my thoughts.

"What do you mean, no we? I intend to help you every step of the way!" I said with determination.

"I shall hunt and kill it, alone. I will not risk the chance of the King's top spiritual advisor and his personal friend becoming an unwilling casualty," she replied flatly.

"Did he not send the both of us on this mission?" I argued. She moved in her seat, shifted her eyes then back to mine.

"You are too old and you move too slowly. Looking after your safety could compromise the outcome."

Well, that rather stung. Stung like sitting on a summer flower occupied by a honey bee. Unfortunately, everything she said was true.

"Yet, there is strength in numbers. Comrades joined together in a common cause... a pack!" I pleaded.

Gadlynn glared to my left and suddenly snapped, "What do you want?"

She did not say it to me. It was to the girl from the street, who appeared as if from out of the shadows.

"I want to agree with the priest. There is value in numbers," she said.

Gadlynn replied once again, sternly, "The Baron offered me his troops in assistance. Why would I deny them, yet take up you two? Some missions are meant to be accomplished alone."

"You would take us in, if you were smart," said the girl.

Gadlynn instantly stood, looking up slightly to meet the girl's face.

"You have been watching us like a hawk since we first arrived. Who are you? And who are you to second guess me? You could be a spy for Falnar for all I know!"

The girl looked angry and intense. I was almost afraid this would escalate into a brawl.

"A spy?" she spat. "Of that, I can assure you I am not! And this hunt you champion has been my hunt, my cause, and as of recently, my entire life's purpose. My name is Darna. And I shall assist you willingly as part of your pack or from afar. Either way, I will be there to see this beast dead."

The girl was determined of mind that much was clear. Gadlynn continued to stare, judging her, sizing her up.

Darna, then, without much thought or common sense offered, "You are shorter than I imagined you would be."

Gadlynn flinched, perhaps suppressing a desire to slug the girl on the chin. This Darna was going to be lying on her backside within mere moments if she persisted with this attitude. Yet Gadlynn surprised me. Perhaps sensing something redeemable about Darna, or something noble, she sat back down.

"I often hear that. The ignorant judge someone's entire worth by height or strength. They soon learn how misguided this is. Time and time again they learn." Gadlynn motioned Darna to pull up a chair. "I won't have you stand there staring down on us like a vulture, sit." Darna looked a little confused, almost confrontational as if considering challenging Gadlynn's request. She relented and sat.

Smart girl.

"Your determination is admirable. You can listen as we plan," Gadlynn conceded.

Finally, with my mind demanding to be unleashed, I spoke up, "As I was wrongfully being denied to partake in this, an idea did occur. Yet Darna, let me first explain: On our way over the pass, a day's ride from here, we had an encounter with a ferocious beast that nearly ended us- or me, at the very least. A bear, an enormous bear, the likes of which I've never seen nor heard of. If not for the precise accuracy of our First Ranger here (Gadlynn nodded at this) this beast would have been dining on monk and mule."

"Which, I assume, would be awfully unpleasant" Gadlynn added...

Thank you for that, Gadlynn.

"If I may continue? Gadlynn's arrows could barely pierce its skin-"

"Perhaps you did not draw back enough?" Darna naively injected.

This poor girl just does not possess any tactful First Ranger conversational diplomacy. Myself, I was quickly and willfully learning to be masterful at this. Who knows? I might even get a positive response from Gadlynn someday.

"I drew back as much as I was able. We were at a full run on horseback," the Ranger defended.

"It might be you need to strengthen your back, for more power in your delivery," Darna said.

"Why am I defending my actions with you?! Did I beckon

you over to join in our discussion?" Gadlynn snapped.

Darna hesitated. "No..."

"No? Well then SHUT IT and let us plan!" Gadlynn motioned for me to continue, hopefully before the girl thought of something else ignorant or inappropriate to add.

"Very well. Without further interruptions, I hope, I shall continue." With that, I cleared my throat and went on, "It is apparent that this thing's hide is like thick, tanned leather. It will take an arrow or bolt of exceptional speed and power to puncture its skin."

"Bolt... hmmm..." Gadlynn pondered. Her hand went up to her chin. I leaned in to further accentuate my presentation.

"The King has a special company of archers that uses crossbows. These crossbows are even able to puncture armor when delivered at a close distance. Now, if we constructed a crossbow... a large crossbow, that just might be sufficient power to penetrate its hide." I slowly sat back, content and humbled by my wisdom.

"I like the idea... what about the latching mechanism and a way of cranking back all that force?" Gadlynn asked.

Fortunately, I had thought this through and suggested, "I recently witnessed a weapons designer's drawings on just such an idea. A cranking wheel allowed for impressive force on the draw.

What I found ingenious was the locking pin: a simple

design really, allowing with every turn of the handle to lock it into position without going forward. Pressing a trigger attached to this pin would release the string, sending the projectile forward with surprising force."

"So, a large crossbow?" Darna said.

I nodded my head in agreement. "Pretty much that, yes"

"Are you confident you could replicate such a device?" Gadlynn asked.

"I could if I had a competent blacksmith to fashion the pin and sprocket" I replied.

Darna perked up, "I know one! A good one, best in town."

"Good," Gadlynn began, "I think this could deliver a-"

"A kill shot!" Darna interjected, happy with herself.

"Yes, a kill shot," said Gadlynn.

"We will need to acquire an incredibly sturdy bow, large enough to do what is required and strong enough not to break. Any suggestions?" I said.

"Ash," Gadlynn supplied, nodding. "Ash is the only wood I know of that could withstand that much pressure... maybe."

"What if it was black ash?" Darna asked, excited.

"Black ash?" Gadlynn asked, with a small, confused frown. "Trees like that do not exist anymore. The most effective bow-making wood ever found- every one I've seen was crafted years a go..."

"One does, and I am the only one who knows where," Darna said defiantly.

"If this is true," I considered, "then we best be about it! We have no time to lose. God forbid another child is taken."

Darna stiffened at my last statement. Her eyes steeled with renewed determination. "Absolutely," she agreed. "I will introduce you to the smithy; you can tell him your designs. Then I will go retrieve this rare wood and, with that, be allowed to join your company."

"If you return with black ash," countered Gadlynn, "I will consider it. No promises. And do your best to keep the tree living-remove only what is needed. Lead us to your blacksmith." And with that, we were off.

Chapter 12

FROM THOUGHT TO CREATION

My time with the blacksmith proved to be very useful. Darna was correct: a very competent craftsman he was. A jolly fellow named Ambaum, thick in the midsection, yet strong in the arms, with a rather large head topped with a thick wave of curly, red hair.

That man knew how to swing a hammer with precision! He put his current project on hold to assist with ours, assuring us that the killing of that beast was at the top of his priorities. So together we fashioned a cranking system, along with a locking release pin.

Now if Darna is able to follow through with her part and is successful in retrieving a large branch of this elusive Black Ash, our Dragon crossbow (I named it such due to the weapon's potential to kill any massive creature, even fictional.) could begin to be assembled. Fortunately for our group, and much due to my encouragement, Ambaum agreed to further assist in its construction.

Later that evening, I found Gadlynn in the archery hall next to the infantry quarters. Quite a crowd of low-level Rangers and soldiers had gathered to observe her practicing. I am thoroughly positive this attention was not by her choice, but rather by the happenstance that one of the best archers in all of Alandora was displaying her skill in their hall. She was impressive, to say the least- center shot after center shot, standing, kneeling and on the move- and the onlookers would applaud often. Concluding her session, she willingly shared tips and strategies with her fellow archers, which they received gladly, I was encouraged to see.

Afterward, we retired back to the inn and engaged with a rather impressive assortment of fine foods, including roast pig and one of my favorites: smashed potatoes with garlic butter spread over the top. Though a dire shadow hung over our evening meal, this was a grand supper indeed. I was especially fond of the part where the innkeeper insisted on no payment and presented me with a rather large glass of Weary Woodsman's finest. A savory vintage producing a most-welcomed numbing effect, taking the edge off the apprehension of the upcoming quest. Just as that edge was getting appreciably dull, Gadlynn raised her head and looked at the door, whispered, "She's returned."

I turned, looking toward the door and saw no one. Facing Gadlynn again I said, "Darna? Are you sure-" I caught myself. Of course she was sure. I quickly added, "I... I sure hope she was successful." Just then, reaffirming Gadlynn's intuitions or whatever they may be, Darna entered and approached.

"I found a branch large enough," she announced proudly. "I was careful sawing; hopefully I did not kill the tree in the process. I left it with Ambaum."

"If we are able to use it and free your village of this nightmare, it will be worth the risk. Lead the way," Gadlynn replied, with a nod.

Excited about the prospect of a weapon that will give us at least some advantage we quickly made our way over to the workshop.

We entered the smithy to find Ambaum laboring away with lanterns and secured candles thoroughly illuminating his work station. It pleased me to see he had contacted the top woodworker in town if not the whole region, I am told- and convinced him to assist in the weapon's fabrication. Wils, an athletic man in his forties, was directly involved in fashioning what I am very pleased to report was indeed Black Ash, carving and preparing the main body of the crossbow. He was hard about it with a wood plane and chisel, shaping on the stock where the bolt will lay.

It was indeed beginning to look like a crossbow. A very large crossbow.

This made me smile.

"Black ash," Gadlynn directed at Darna. "I thought I would

never see this day. You have performed well."

The young ranger aspirant looked down in humility; it was probably Darna's first encounter with this characteristic.

"Thank you, First Ranger."

Gadlynn looked from Darna over to Ambaum. "Ambaum, might I have a word in private?" she said. They moved to the other side of the shop, out of hearing range for Darna, yet not for this curiously-minded monk. She continued, "The monk and I appreciate your diligent work on the crossbow."

"Why, of course! Anything to help bring about an end to that creature, you can count on me."

I saw Gadlynn's eyes dart our way for a moment before flitting back. "I wanted to ask you: how well do you know Darna?"

Ambaum looked surprised by the nature of the question, replying," Why, I've known Darna her whole life! I'm good friends with her parents, Jon and Marta. Jon grows some of the best corn this side of Greensdale; he gives me and Gerta a few bushels for free every harvest. Very fine folk indeed!"

"Hmmm. The reason I ask," said Gadlynn, lowering her voice further, and near to the limit of my hearing, "is that Darna is absolutely insistent on joining this hunt. I just can't go about risking the life of someone for a quest bestowed upon me-"

"Gadlynn," Ambaum interjected, "I think I can shed some

light on this for you." He took in a deep breath and then continued, "There is a very good reason Darna is so motivated about your 'quest,' because it has been her quest for the last year. That creature killed Darna's sister... Alena was her name. One of its first victims. Her and Wils' boy, Bradon." Gadlynn's mouth opened. Things were beginning to make sense.

Ambaum looked over at Wils, resolutely working away. He continued, "You should have seen Wils when I approached him about your bow idea. He literally dropped what he was doing and followed me over. 'Anything to bring about vengeance on that Hellspawn,' he said. Darn good craftsman; he'll make you the best crossbow you've ever seen."

"Of that I have no doubt... Ambaum, if Darna were to get injured or killed in this hunt, her parents would be devastated…I don't know if I can allow the possibility of that happening," Gadlynn pleaded.

"I will tell you this right now, if she was to be left out of this hunt, that would devastate her for the rest of her young life. Gadlynn, she blames herself for Alena's death. She allowed her to go that night to meet with Bradon- she didn't interfere and has never forgiven herself. Yes, Darna's got blood in this, her and Wils both... ah hells below, the whole town's got blood in this! If something happens to one of us, it happens to all of us, that is the way of Greensdale."

Gadlynn pondered a moment, seeming to soak it all in. For my part, I was sympathetic and understanding of the pain and frustration both Darna and Wils must be feeling. How could we deny her a chance at revenge? Yet, what if she gets killed in the process?

So many variables. So many different possibilities and outcomes.

God grant Gadlynn insight.

The moon was high into the night sky, and I, for one, welcomed when Gadlynn told everyone to go home and rest. Tomorrow's another day, and perhaps at the end of the week this weapon will be ready for testing. The response, however, was surprising. The three of them- Darna, Ambaum and Wils- grew incredibly somber and it was Wils who delicately spoke up, "Miss First Ranger, I reckon I would just assume to carry on with this task, if it's all the same? I just need... to keep busy, keep working and see it done."

The others nodded in agreement and did not stir from their stations. They had cause as justified as any, and with that, clarity of purpose. Gadlynn and I looked at them and witnessed a unit, single-minded and resolute, with a bond forged by fire. We were all on the same mission but they had nightmares to overcome. And little by little, as they toiled away, they came that much closer to their personal horror arriving at a closure.

They needed this outlet and they needed to share this time with each other. Gadlynn and I recognized this and graciously bowed out.

"We look forward to seeing you in the morning," Gadlynn offered.

With a little zeal I added, "You are some of the finest craftsmen in Alandora, and soon... soon this beast will get a taste of revenge!"

They wholeheartedly agreed, echoing my sentiment by adding, their voices in unison, "Revenge!"

Gadlynn and I slipped out into the night. We soon found our way back to the Weary Woodsmen, bid a good evening, and retired to our rooms. I promptly began noting in my journal- I wanted to dictate the day's event thoroughly and accurately while my mind was still, somewhat fresh. After several pages were filled and the ink already dry, I found myself nodding off.

The next morning, I awoke there at my desk, my head on my arms. I slept well yet my back was rather stiff and, oh yes, wouldn't you know it, a rather large smear of ink down my hand. I do hope that washes out, perhaps not? Maybe I should wear it as a badge of honor.

***

"Wash your face and hands in ink this morning, monk?" Gadlynn asked. "Normally one uses water and what they call wash soap. "

I was confused. We had been sitting there enjoying fried eggs and thick-cut strips of bacon and she suddenly mentions this?

Noticing some fine glass dining ware in a cabinet, I quickly rose and positioned myself to see my face in its reflection. Not only were my hands smeared with ink, half my face was also. No wonder the innkeeper's host snickered when I first arrived. Ahh, the price one pays for falling asleep on the job.

I soon returned to my room and washed away my past transgressions, praying, for fear of continued embarrassment especially from her- that my scrubbing was thorough enough.

Looking at my desk, I was relieved to see that in my slumber I did not destroy any of my filled pages, only one I partially started. It takes thought and effort to put notes to paper; how disheartening it would have been to have wasted time and effort, smearing the night's work simply for yielding to the sandman.

A loud knock on my door jarred my thoughts. "Let's get going, we don't have all day," came Gadlynn's muffled voice.

I quickly grabbed my staff and met her in the Hall, and the

two of us hurried over to Ambaums.

It was clear from Gadlynn's expression when we arrived that she shared my surprised reaction: all three of Greensdale's elite (this strictly my opinion) were still laboring away, with what appeared to be an inexhaustible focus, on the weapon's completion. It was a couple of hours after dawn and they're still here? Toiling throughout the entire nighttime? Impressive was their dedication to this cause.

The heat from the furnace was most welcome after the cool morning air. Ambaum noticed us and quickly called us over and began explaining their progress.

"Come look at this," he said proudly, holding up the main body.

"Grooved and drilled. The winch and release pin perform just as you designed! We've sampled it, the mechanisms all work." I was relieved. to see my idea, even though this was not entirely my idea, be designed, constructed, assembled, AND to have it actually working... exuberance!

Ambaum continued, "Darna is creating a bowstring that should be able to withstand the incredible tension that drawing the crossbow will create."

Darna looked up for a moment, acknowledging us with a nod.

"She has combined three strings into one; we think it should hold true. If you come over here, Wils is working the bow section. This is where the strength and integrity of the black ash will be most effective: all of the weapon's potential will depend on this wood's ability to bend and recoil without breaking."

Wils held up his masterpiece for us to examine, and remarkable it was!

"Normally," Wils began, "I would spend weeks drying and treating the bow, but time is of the essence. We can't risk that thing claiming anymore lives, so I've been hardening it with Ambaum's furnace. I'm pretty sure this will work."

I was more than impressed, I could see Gadlynn was also.

"Outstanding... superb, to say the least. Do you think," I ventured, "that a trial run will be possible in two days' time?" Wils and Ambaum shared a look and then the blacksmith spoke up, "Two days' time? We were thinking more like this afternoon. That is, if you are willing?"

If we are willing? I could not help but laugh inside. Their efforts have been extraordinary; the King himself could not have asked for more dedication.

"How about late afternoon?" said Gadlynn. "You could all do with a meal or two and some sleep." She looked at each and added, "You have done your people and our King proud... beyond compare."

She walked out after that, clearly satisfied with this weapon's potential and the capable hands constructing it.

"Well done, everyone, well done indeed. Shall we meet around three?" I offered.

They waved me off with affirmation, intent on resuming the various tasks they were involved with.

I smiled, nodded, and exited. It is satisfying to know that in this vast, massive world we live in, filled with wars, greed and other vile things fueled by evil intentions, that other good people do exist. These righteous folks, weighed down by all sorts of interference and interruptions of some calamity or another, still willing to sacrifice precious time from their plight to lend a hand assisting their fellow neighbor in need.

Lord teach me to be more selfless... just like them.

- As the First Ranger and I approached Ambaum's smithy a little before three, Gadlynn noticed a commotion off to the rear of the building. We walked towards the sounds and saw Wil happy as a second serving of apple pie, jumping up and down, exclaiming, "I knew it would work! Heavens above, I knew it!"

He turned his head our way, noticed us, and with exaggerated gyrations motioned us over.

"Gadlynn, and the monk fella-"

"It's Brother Matthew" I supplied with humble, spiritual indignation.

"Ah, yes, Brother Matt, well, gather around and witness a weapon of war the likes all of Alandora has never seen!

How thrilling, I thought, apparently Wils was so excited he couldn't fathom waiting for a group trial. All the better, I say, to have the ones who did most of the work reap the joys of its success.

Darna walked up to Gadlynn with a- no?... yes!- a smile. She was eager to share with her and said, "The black ash held true, what power it produces!"

"This is good news!" Gadlynn replied. "What are you using for projectiles? Arrows or bolts? And I was under the impression we were going to meet at three, after you all had rested." Darna looked down. I believe she even kicked a small rock away. I guess that is the "go-to" motion when being admonished.

"About that... well... we all just continued working and-" "All of us realized we lost track of time," Ambaum interjected.

"Also realized that not one of us would have been able to sleep. Our hearts would have been right here, so we just kept at it... though we did slip in some tea and cakes my wife brought in. That helped renew our aspirations."

It was a most welcome interruption, by the look of Darna's

face.

"I for one, cannot and will not fault you for your determination and your... passion," said Gadlynn, to the relief of the others. "I just wish that you would have... no. This is a good moment for Greensdale. Look at you now, all of you have sacrificed much for this moment. It is all good and it is all well. Ambaum, Wils... Darna, shall we see what she can do?" The others grew excited and began preparing the crossbow. It was rather large, as I mentioned, yet not as heavy as one would expect, most likely due to the quality of the Black Ash. Still, it was awkward, so they had constructed a two-legged stand where the weapon could be propped up, still able to pivot and aim.

Ambaum grabbed one of his custom-made bolts, fashioned from steel, saying, "We had tried a few larger wooden arrows, but we were not getting the results we had hoped, so I wanted to try something made out of metal. I've been working on a fancy, decorative gate for Lord Bisbee. He lives outside of Arverd a lil' to the north. This gate he is wanting has long, thin metal poles on much of it. Since he hasn't paid me a blasted coin as of yet, I reckon I would at least 'borrow' a few poles, courtesy of Bisbee... look at this-"

Ambaum held up a thin, sturdy metal bolt. It stood about three feet long and was very sharp on one end. The other end was notched in the center, I assume to keep the string from slipping off. He motioned Wils over to help, and the two of them made sure the crossbow was securely perched on their makeshift stand.

"Now, prepare yourselves to be impressed," said Ambaum.

Wils laughed and added, "The Good Lord knows I was!" Ambaum steadied the bow on the stand and began cranking the handle, tightening the string. When he reached what he felt was a strong enough pull, he latched it secure with the pin. "Now place a bolt in there, Darna."

She eagerly loaded a bolt onto the groove and then stepped back.

"Good. Now see the stump? Watch..." Ambaum said.

A notched-up tree stump sat in the ground a good thirty paces away. Ambaum elevated his aim a little high on purpose, compensating for a slight drop due to distance and bolt weight.

We held our breath, hoping for a positive result.

WOOOSH! He pulled the trigger, launching the bolt forward, ferociously slicing through the air.

SLAM!

The bolt impacted near the center, hitting the stump so violently that we actually felt it under our feet.

"WOOHOOO!" Wils yelled, proceeding again to dance about with his indescribable gyrations. This prompted joyous reactions from all of us... except Gadlynn.

She walked over to the stump and stared at it for a spell before attempting to pull out the bolt. It would not budge. She tried again with the same result, then slowly turned towards us. As she did, her intense glare faded a bit and then her mouth transitioned into a smile. The kind of smile that says, "Yes, oh yes... this creature is going to die!"

We all cheered. It was a grand moment, a heady payoff for the countless hours of work and effort poured into the weapon's creation. It pierced through the blanketing depression and fear that had been slowly smothering me since it became clear that we, (hopefully we) , would be returning to that hellspawn's lair, and now, at last, I felt confident of success.

Now I need only convince her of my place in the hunt. No easy task, this one...

All of us walked up to the stump, boasting about the penetration and impact the crossbow produced. In this positive atmosphere, I felt that my deliberations on why I should be joined in her quest would be better received. I silently emboldened my inner courage and proceeded, "Gadlynn, I would ask you to reconsider my participation in the hunt. My strength might be put to good use handling the crossbow and I- "

"Could help steady it," she finished. "And also assist

packing it in since we will have no horses that close to the fray." My face slowly formed a grin. I was not sure why I was smiling exactly, willingly joining in a hunt that would most likely allow me yet another opportunity to sup tea with Death- and somehow rationalize again why now is not the right time to take a most unwelcome extended walk with him.

"And Darna," Gadlynn continued, causing Darna to perk up, listening intently, "You have convinced me of your passion and commitment. Ambaum has shared with me your past and why this is so important to you. In your boots, I would feel the same. I will allow you to join me and Brother Matthew - IF..." She paused, intently looking into Darna's eyes as if sensing her reaction and ability to respond in truth.

"If?" Darna echoed.

"*If* you are willing to follow orders. Follow orders without questioning my authority or my reasons," Gadlynn demanded.

"But what if I-" Darna objected- foolishly, I might add. Oh the youth of today, will they ever learn?

"There are no 'what ifs.' Either you are capable of following my orders without comment, or you are not. And if you are not, I will bind you to a tree until we return."

"You wouldn't da-"

"Dare? Try me." The First Ranger stood face to face with

Darna. The threat she just leveled was for two very important reasons as far as I could see. One, Darna needs to be put in her place or it could possibly be detrimental to our journey and its outcome. Two, Darna needs to be put in her place... oops...oh my, did I just mention that?

I guess some statements are worth repeating. Darna backed down, wisely.

"I can follow orders..."

"Without questions." Gadlynn insisted.

"Yes, without questions," Darna mumbled reluctantly.

"Very well then. I will hold you to it. Your words have been witnessed by everyone here, so you are now held accountable for your actions," said Gadlynn.

"I understand," Darna said. "I will not disappoint you or the good Brother here."

"You will be a most welcome comrade on our quest," I added.

"Thank you," she replied.

Gadlynn looked the group over and said,"The three of us will practice handling and shooting the crossbow. We need to be fluent in its operation. Also, Darna and I will work our archery until dark. I do have a plan, but in order for this to succeed, we need to work as a team- one group, single-minded. I shall tell you this plan tomorrow; for now, let us practice."

So we did, we shot, reloaded, and shot countless times more. I could operate that bow in my sleep. I think that was Gadlynn's very intention: to make us so familiar that the chance for failure would be considerably minimized. At dusk, we were ready to retire. Every moment not spent hunting this creature down and extinguishing it could be another opportunity for it to wreak havoc and perhaps claim another victim. Gadlynn decided that the three of us were to meet before dawn and set off, light load, horses and weaponry only. (Sorry Florence! Trust me, you're better off eating hay in your stable).

"I sure wish Ambaum and I could join you tomorrow. We could be of good use to you," said Wils.

"I am positive the both of you would do yourselves proud," Gadlynn replied, "yet I am already taking along two more than I originally intended." She patted the crossbow and added, "Besides, you have more than proven yourselves in this mission by providing us with... an edge."

They apparently liked hearing that. Smiling and slapping each other on the back. Wils spoke up, "I've been meaning to ask you, how are we to know for certain it is this creature, this Bear that is the one responsible for..." He took in a deep breath, but could not continue, tears forming around the edges of his eyes.

"After we kill it," spoke Gadlynn, "we shall search its lair. We will bring torches. Hopefully we can find some evidence to help us determine if this beast is the one to blame."

I could judge by her actions the past couple of days that she was awfully convinced this monstrosity of a bear was the guilty one. How she knew this, who can say? This is Gadlynn Wayfare we're talking about.

Darna hugged her two workmates, bid us farewell until morning, then disappeared into the darkness down some trail only a local would know anything about. Ambaum and Wils looked at us both intently, as if it might be the last time they would see us.

"All of you come back safe and sound, even if it's to come back and fight another day... be prudent." Ambaum said.

"Aye, and remember: you won't be able to outrun this thing, so your aim better be true," Wils added.

"At my speed, it is our only chance!" I replied impulsively, attempting to keep everyone's spirits up. They chuckled, yet it was Gadlynn who bested me-

"Brother Matthew, if we do get chased again, I only need be quicker than you," the First Ranger stated.

It took just a moment for everyone to absorb what she said. Then they burst into laughter and slapped me on the back a few times.

I reckon it does not pay to be the slowest in a party of three being chased by a bear. It was a most welcome release, on the cusp of such a dire undertaking.

They followed up by wishing us their best and demanded that we return in the best of health and also flaunting one large bear head. Gadlynn agreed, politely bowed and retreated toward the inn; the others returned to the smithy to close the shop down for the night. While I stood there watching Ambaum and Wils walk away, I could not help but think what good and decent people these Greensdale folks were. I pray we are successful. After all they have been through, it wouldn't do to disappoint them.

No, Lord, it wouldn't do at all.

Chapter 13

ON WITH THE HUNT!

The three of us gathered prior to sunrise and soon made our way toward the Mt. Goor pass. Travel was difficult; darkness mixed with fog impeded our progress. If not for Gadlynn's keen sight and natural sense of direction, Darna and I most certainly would have slipped off the roadway in one unpleasant fashion or another. So we willingly followed her lead, trusting in her superb navigational skills. Bitter and I were loaded with the dissembled crossbow and all its mounting hardware. It was quite bulky, and thankfully it was hauled more by Bitter than I.

All pieces were meticulously fastened down so as not to clank or clamor- Gadlynn wanted absolute silence, no need announcing our arrival or exposing our intentions. On this, I wholeheartedly agreed. Now was not the time for idle chit chat or taking any risk whatsoever. As she explained to us earlier, we must all be of a single mind and of a single purpose. Our only focus will be on complete fulfillment and success of our mission: the absolute destruction of this hell-beast.

Before we left, I was pleased to see Florence displayed

very little disappointment about not attending our quest. She seemed content to stay in her stall munching away on hay and barley. Out of all of us during the chase, it was poor Florence who was the closest to being bear food; I feel it is only fair she is allowed to sit this one out. We shall return before too long, faithful one. .. God willing.

The air grew colder as we gained elevation. We could see the sun attempting to break through in between mountain peaks. I did wish it would hurry; these cold bones of mine were in desperate need of some warming. In time, the darkness had no choice but to recede as light began its journey into day, slowly expanding its wings throughout the mountainside. I began to recognize sections of roadway that we had recently encountered on our hurried route to Greensdale. I was now able to distinguish certain landmarks, such as unusually shaped boulders or massive, uniquely formed trees, some standing and other ill-fortuned ones not.

Such is the way of life, I thought. Through time, storm, or disease, these once enormous timbers now lay decaying on the forest floor, unable to contest the hand of time decomposing their wooden corpses back into the earth. Hopefully, to soon reemerge as a new sapling, giving life another go.

Before we had agreed to this task, I was going to

recommend avoiding the Mt. Goor pass all together and considering another route back to the castle, thus we could possibly avoid another encounter with you-know-who. Now, that idea is all for naught.

Hopefully, by next day tomorrow, this section of pass will be cleared; no need to reroute this roadway for us... nor for anyone. Look at us, servants of the people...

As we drew nearer, it was difficult not allowing apprehension to creep its way into my thinking. It was becoming challenging simply to breathe- was that due to the elevation, or the task at hand? Either way, it was here that Gadlynn raised her hand.

We immediately stopped, and surveyed the woods around us.

She slid down Blackwing and approached us. She whispered, "The lair is around the bend and east, through the trees. We walk the horses here forward. Darna, equip your bow and nock an arrow. If it attacks, remember, draw back as far as you're able. We need power to penetrate its hide." Gadlynn had an arrow nocked on her bow before I was able to blink. With her other hand she led Blackwing forward.

Darna nodded. She had taken on a serious tone since we gathered early this morning; gone was that rebellious attitude of hers that we were accustomed to battling. That constant challenge to everything and everyone who was in authority, thankfully, was temporarily on hold. Darna was no different than other late-teens her age, yet the seriousness of this moment demanded that childish manners be put aside. She knew she had to rise to the occasion. This was the day she had likely been praying for since Alena's death, the day and time she would deliver retribution. Above all else, Darna had to make this opportunity count. She climbed down and drew her bow, looking calm, yet it was easy for me to notice signs of trepidation.

If my heart wasn't pumping blood to my head so rapidly, I would have remembered to give her a look of confidence, a head nod of reinforcement, anything to foster encouragement. Yet the moment had passed as I dismounted Bitter, and began following Gadlynn's lead. Darna will be admirable and make this moment count, of this I am confident. She will rise to this occasion or be remembered as the comrade who on this day helped exact vengeance and regain sense and order throughout Greensdale and the lands surrounding.

Make us proud, Darna.

Soon we approached the clearing, that foreboding stretch of forest I did my best to forget, yet was physically unable to.

Such horrific places as these, delivering such traumatic events, burned deep, leaving everlasting imprints in your mind. It certainly has with me. I was shaking, looking around at the dense forest and the area Gadlynn came rushing from. She motioned for me to tie off my horse and prepare the crossbow. I began unfastening all the strapping that held it bundled together, and before long it lay unwrapped before me. Gadlynn gestured for me to continue, so I began its assembly immediately. Along the outer edges of my vision I saw Darna, bow in hand, scanning the area and guarding our position.

Gadlynn still held her bow with her left hand, an arrow firmly held between her fingers, ready to be drawn. In her other hand was a large bag, the contents of which I wasn't able to determine. Whatever it was, it had a foul scent about it.

The crossbow was finally ready for use. I quietly returned the hand tools to their bag. Arranging the two-legged stand, I propped it up underneath the bow's weight. It felt good in my hands. The lethality of this device was staggering. We are going to deliver ol' brown fur one "How do you do?" and "Good morning" he'll never forget.

I looked over and nodded at Gadlynn. She was scanning in the direction of the lair. Her focus was intense; I could tell she was attempting that smelling or intuition thing she does.

Darna moved in close as I whispered to Gadlynn, "Is it up there? Do you smell it?"

“It is there. Still... yet like before, there is something strange about it... hard to explain. Its scent is peculiar. Different than other bears. I am unfamiliar with this. But, yes, it is up there.”

I would rather not add more fear upon myself, and especially at this particular moment- the moment right before we walk into the mouth of Hell. Yet something seeming peculiar, coming from her, gives me pause to be even more concerned. Not only were my hands freely shaking, but my legs began to feel weak, even trembling.

A touch from Gadlynn shook me from my anxiety, “Brother... focus. You are strong; it is up to you to haul that bow up the hill. I will point out where you set up,” she said quietly. Then Gadlynn, recognizing the desperate need Darna and I had for inspiration, added, “There is good news. The wind is blowing toward us. The beast will have a harder time knowing we’re here.”

That’s at least a little encouragement, I thought. At this stage I’ll take all I can receive. Gadlynn checked each of the horses to make sure they were tethered correctly. She had explained to us earlier that they should be tied in such a way that, if spooked, could not easily break free, yet quickly unleashed if we were chased. Satisfied, she put her finger to her mouth for absolute quiet and began walking forward into the thick, lush green of the woodland hillside. She was stealthy like a cat, practically silent, and very impressive to see. Darna followed close behind, trying to approximate her motions, yet was not as effective as our First Ranger.

I, on the other hand, after watching these two attentively maneuver through the brush, felt like a lumbering giant incapable of controlling its limbs. Every attempt to minimize noise by side stepping away from a dead branch only resulted in my large feet stepping on a full pile of crispy dried leaves.

Not even slightly helpful for trying to be quiet. Gadlynn motioned me to take each step slow, and so I did. The hillside was laced with large fir trees and all sorts of various underbrush, resulting in one tired monk in a very short time period. I became very heated; sweat began channeling down my forehead. Yet upward we went, our purpose could wait no longer.

- After what seemed like a lifetime, Gadlynn suddenly raised her fist. Even in my near-fatally-exerted state, ready to welcome physical collapse, I recognized I was to instantly stop and remain absolutely silent. She signaled us to squat down, her keen gaze scouring the treeline above us. She then crept over to me, motioning Darna to join us.

"The lair is above the next rise," Gadlynn whispered.

"Get your wind back and drink some water. I still feel its presence."

I was not sure if that was reassuring to hear or dreadful. Either way, before too long I found my wind again and nodded to Gadlynn for us to proceed. She lifted her hand upward; we slowly arose in unison, connecting ourselves with her fluid movement. Once again she pressed forward, in complete harmony with the forest, hardly a sound made. Some fortunate folks, like Darna and especially Gadlynn, were just gifted with a natural grace. I certainly was not.

We maneuvered our way through congested stands of massive fir trees, our only defense if in need of escape. (Thank you, Lord, for large trees!) Soon the three of us, through the vertical columns of timber and low-lying underbrush, were able to witness the abomination that was the creature's lair. It looked as if it were the very entrance to Hades. I do believe, at that very moment, everyone in our party struggled with second thoughts: our souls beckoning us to reconsider and end this foolish quest.

I don't want to go to hell and I will not go to hell, yet today, we are to knock on its door and await a reply from the master of the house. What a dreadful scene we gazed upon... beyond the security of our beloved firs, the hillside flattened out and gave way to a ragged ravine, lined with boulders and void of foliage. This ravine lead straight into a massive black opening into the earth; as far as I could tell this was a pathway to the underworld.

Near this entrance, I was able to make out odd shapes... stones protruding from the ground in unnatural randomness. Yet these white stones, upon further examination, were not stones at all... but bones. Bones, both animals and humans alike. I was able to discern this by the skulls--it was hard from this distance to distinguish any other bone from another. Incredibly disheartening. The only evidence remaining of some unfortunate soul's existence just lay there, decaying away like that of old trees. This lair was not so much a home for some beast as it was a tomb for its victims.

Gadlynn waved and caught my eye. She motioned for me to set up directly in line of the opening, a few feet in front of two large trees. From this standpoint I would have a straight shot into the cave's opening and into the beast when it reveals itself. I situated myself where she directed and quietly unfolded the stand. I firmly secured it in its position and afterward attached the crossbow with Ambaum's cleverly designed latches. Relieved that the bow was fastened properly without generating too much noise, I slowly rotated the handle, producing impressive tension on the string. When I felt pleased with the draw, I quickly secured the locking pin. Lastly, I reached into my bag and carefully handled one of Ambaum's lethal metal bolts, securely placing it in the crossbow's groove.

Glancing over every piece of this weapon's hardware and

function, I mentally verified all was in place. Satisfied, I searched deep within myself for some inner "hero" to provide me with temporary courage. Lord, be near! I finally inhaled a deep breath of cool mountain air (unfortunately laced with the noticeable stench from that beast's lair). If there was ever a time to proceed with this foolhardy business, it was now. I shared my readiness visually with Gadlynn.

Beforehand, the two of them stood guard over me; now she motioned for Darna to set up to my left, where she tactically concealed herself behind a stout fir trunk. Gadlynn, with both bow and bag in hand, crept, catlike, closer to the opening along the rocky ravine wall to my right. She slowly opened up her bag and produced what appeared to be a large bloody hind section of lamb.

The Ranger quickly made eye contact with the both of us, reaffirming our readiness, then silently stood and, with a hearty swing, lobbed the raw meat into the cave entrance.

Nothing happened.

We stood at the ready, waiting for the inevitable attack, yet this creature stirred not. Gadlynn crept back into a better position, arrow notched, bow taut. Still, nothing.

My hand shook and I felt the warmth of a thin line of sweat creeping its way down my forehead. Even from my position, I could hear Darna's heartbeat, pounding in her chest... upon second thought, I am pretty certain that was my own.

Gadlynn suddenly lurched to her side, pointing her bow to the top of the rocky hillside-

"TO THE RIGHT!!!!" she screamed. Instantaneous mayhem erupted. The massive beast rose up and over the west hillside with blazing speed and a ferocity I am convinced no other creature could emulate. It did not stand and proudly roar threats, exposing itself- no, it instantly pursued us as adversaries.

How I did not hear it approach until this very moment, I will never know. As of this moment my mind and senses had practically shut down from shock and fear.

Gadlynn bounded down the rocks like a deer, the beast right behind her. An arrow streaked by on my left; Darna's hopefully finding a home in its hide somewhere. I tried to rotate the crossbow to intercept the beast, yet as I did, Gadlynn ran by in front of me with the bear immediately behind. I was not sure if she intentionally did this, but it was the quickest path to the firs.

Its enormous bulk charged past me. I could swear it barely brushed me, yet the bow and I were hurled skyward. As my feet flew up above me, I watched the bolt launch free from the bow and disappear. I landed hard and heard a loud crunch. Stunned, I was unable to breath or move. I was, however, able to discern the sound of the beast pursuing Gadlynn- or Darna, or both, most likely.

How it did not pounce on me when it went by is another mystery; perhaps it recognized Gadlynn's scent from before and sought to exact its revenge first on her. One thing was certain: my comrades needed me right then and there. I had to regain my senses and take up the fight. Shaking my head free of confusion, I rolled onto my side and stood. Nothing felt broken... on me.

The bow was another issue. The stand legs were in pieces.

A scream captured my attention, and though I could see them not, the direction of the commotion through the forest was obvious from where I stood.

"Run through the trees!" Gadlynn screamed. There was fear

in her voice- a most unusual characteristic in her, I am sure. It was only a matter of moments before the creature would best them in some way or another.

Dread filled me. I had to help... I had to do something!

I frantically looked about, trying to determine what I could do to help kill this hell-spawn. I glanced down and saw the crossbow laying upside down upon the forest floor. I assumed it was broken, just like the stand, yet with newfound hope, I discovered that the weapon appeared operational! Although incredibly heavy and awkward, I found untapped strength and was able to handle it as if it were normal sized. I searched through the surrounding ferns and soon spotted the sack, from which I hurriedly retrieved a much-coveted bolt and ran towards the fray. Upon my first step I realized that my knee was injured, and I recognized the familiar warmth of blood. Yet, I ignored it. I must.

Every step, my body demanded that I stop, yet necessity outweighed practicality and I forced myself forward. In the distance I was pleased to see both Gadlynn and Darna still alive, although the situation was tenuous at best. Separate from each other, they did their best to draw back as far as they were able and sink their arrows into the hind quarters of the beast while its attention was pursuing the other.

This was one of Gadlynn's strategies, should this particular situation develop. I was pleased to see it was having an effect.

The creature's movement was noticeably hindered. Up ahead I spied a clearing where I might position myself for a potential shot. Grimacing with each step, I made my way forward. Lumbering giant or not, I was no longer concerned about making noise, just of sinking a bolt deep within the bear's hide.

I reached the top of a small rise above them. I could see the women below me, noble in their efforts, dodging attacks and using the large trees to deflect and shield them from any swipes from its deadly paws. Dear Lord in Heaven, that bear was massive. Its roar, its aggression, was enough to make me want to curl up and tremble like an infant. Its dagger-like claws tore deep into the bark of the trees as easily as if they were flesh. God forbid if one of those were to find its mark. In hindsight I should have grabbed two bolts, yet there was no time for second guessing, I must make this one shot count. I quickly cranked back the handle and latched the pin into position. With all the shoulder strength I could gather, I held it upright and secured the bolt in place.

"Kill it, Monk!" Gadlynn screamed. Darna was firing arrows into the beast's back legs as the First Ranger scampered between firs. That thing's back end must have had twelve arrows protruding from it; it was astounding that it could move at all.

Yet still it raged on, charging and attacking with

unreasoning fury. Absolutely frightening. From this angle, my shot could easily miss- that could not happen, our lives depended on it. I needed to get closer. Shocks of pain riddled my knee as I climbed down over sharp boulders and between ferns. The roar of that creature was deafening. I greatly desired to cover my ears and end its nightmarish bellowing. Yet I persisted, and finally within range, I muscled up the bow, attempting to aim as best I could. Now if it would only be so kind as to stay still for one moment! This creature was determined, driven beyond comprehension. It had no intention of losing the battle this day, so it did not acquiesce to my wish, no, it turned from my fellow comrades and charged ME.

Insanely consumed with an uncontrollable bloodlust, the beast ran toward me, unstoppable, its muscles rippling with each step.

My resolve melted quicker than a late spring snow overcome by sunlight. I felt as if I morphed into a statue, incapable of responding, so mesmerized was I. This beast would not be denied.

A massive wave of brown fur and flesh charged forward,

unrelenting, steam and drool flowing from its gaping mouth of sharp teeth, it's black empty eyes only saw me...

... and I, in return, looked upon Death.

***

- A round, wooden table held just enough room for the two of us. A dainty porcelain tea cup twinkled enticingly on the saucer before me, steam and an alluring aroma wafting from the contents within.

Across from me it sat. Content and completely at ease. A bone-white hand lifted a cup to its lips and I heard a sip, yet saw no face. A large tattered, black robe covered its entirety.

A menacing scythe stood behind it, leaning against a cold rock wall. A sober reminder of the stakes at hand.

"Are you finally ready for a taste? I prepared this especially for you," Death spoke.

I was unable to derive a source from which it spoke, so dark and hidden its face. An instinctive self-preserving reaction was to be my immediate response... yet I held back. This was not the right setting for half-witted instantaneous replies and banter.

No, to bypass, to return from this situation would require more thought... more cunning.

"Normally, I would more than welcome the opportunity to sample a unique blend of tea and spices- especially originating from your peculiar sources." I quickly drew in air and continued, "yet fortunately, prior to our current undertaking- which I am positive has captivated your current attention- I consumed more than a fair portion of both breakfast and morning teas." Death stirred not, and simply replied, “I labored brewing you this special blend and you presume to deny me?”

“With all due respect, yes... for you see, the setting at your fine table is... incorrect,” I revealed. I spread my arms in a broad gesture, dramatizing my point further. “You have only prepared two servings, you need four.”

“I was not aware of additional... guests,” Death puzzled.

“That is where you have erred. You see, without my return, you will need enough tea for not only myself, but for my comrades as well,” I challenged and continued, “For without my last effort, tragedy will certainly over take all on this day. Have you seen this beast?”

“I have,” Death intoned, offering no empathy, nor emotion. Not the most gregarious of persons, this one.

Perhaps at this moment I had the rest of eternity to await his response, for that is what it seemed... until finally “We shall meet again... soon,” Death stated, all too clearly for my liking.

“Of that, I have no doubt,” I said, and as I leaned back in my chair -

***

-I fell back against the rocky hillside. The crossbow, shaking in my hands from both its weight and my overwhelming fear, was angled upward. If not for the debilitating shots from our archers, the beast most certainly would have overtaken me, yet just as it readied to pounce, Gadlynn landed an arrow in its flank.

Apparently it was effective, because the bear suddenly stopped and reared upward, exposing its chest.

I pulled the trigger. The force of the bolt's release jolted my entire frame.

What followed was a sickening scream the likes of which will ever haunt my dreams. The beast arched up in anguish; steam, blood and spittle flew from its maw. Red overtook the brown in the fur surrounding the bolt in its chest. As I lay back against the hillside, not knowing if I should attempt to rise and run, I found I was once again frozen, forced to witness the bear's struggle and confusion as it discovered it was hopelessly incapable of correcting its predicament. I watched for what seemed an eternity until, finally, with a last release of breath, it signaled defeat, collapsing forward, its weight shoving the bolt in further.

I had just witnessed, and partaken in, the finality of this unspeakable horror.

Chapter 14

A MATTER OF CONCLUSIONS

I lay back, resting upon the rocky ground, and although it was littered with uncomfortable stones and fir branches, I cared not. I at last allowed fatigue to have its say. My knee throbbed, fresh blood continuing to spread across my pant leg.

Stunned and beyond exhausted, I simply tried to focus on breathing and allow the reality of our success to register. Soft movement through brush announced the arrival of my fellow comrades.

"Matthew, are you well? Did the beast bite you?" Gadlynn asked.

They stood above me, looking down, not yet knowing how to assess my state. Quick glances at the massive mound of ratty, brown fur close by signaled that none of us were quite convinced that the bear was actually dead. Although I did not want to look at the beast, or see its angry, hideous bulk again, I sat up and made sure--no rise of its body, no air being sucked in and out. It lay still, and that was all well with me.

"Matthew, speak to me. Are you well?" Gadlynn insisted. I

have to admit, I was not myself. I was completely dazed and disoriented, yet I forced myself to sift through my mental fog and converse.

"I am well," I replied. "It is dead, Gadlynn, it is... dead."

"That it is, thanks to all of us and especially that expert shot of yours. You might want to consider joining the Rangers," she said.

I could not help but smile. To hear a compliment from her was rare- rare indeed.

"Did the beast bite or touch you in any way?" she continued.

"No... I ache all over, but all this blood," I said, pointing to my knee, "is from my fall."

"Good. Because I figured out what was peculiar about its scent, what was so strange and unfamiliar... It is... was... sick...

Sick in its head. Diseased." She pointed at the creature, a mere ten feet from us. "See its mouth? All that white foam and spittle? It was rabid, like a dog from a place infested, who eats too much spoiled food."

Darna walked over to the dead bear, stared for a bit then kicked it, hard.

"Disease or not," she screamed, "rot in hell, beast!"

No explanation could have soothed the hurt of losing her

sister to its primal desire.

"Let's go to its lair and look for evidence," Darna demanded.

"No, let us rest," Gadlynn insisted gently. "We have just defeated what many in the village believed we could not, including Baron Arlo."

"But the-"

"We rest," she said, firmer. That was the end of it, and Darna sat down next to me. She was starting to learn.

Gadlynn went and circled the creature, as I marveled at its size. Darna and I just sat and watched her as she approached its humongous head. Myself, I am blessed with a rather large head able to hold more wisdom, my mother used to say. This bear's head must have been three times bigger than my own.

Humbling. You wouldn't think it possible, but there it lay right in front of us. Thank you Lord; I am so relieved that it is dead and we... still live.

No tea today, Death.

Gadlynn pulled out her short sword. She flipped the blade into her hand, squatted down, and tapped the top of the bears cranium with the pommel. It was solid bone, no different from stone. She shook her head in amazement before standing to face us. And then in a rare moment, Gadlynn began to speak at length.

"When I first took over the leadership of the Rangers, it was not by choice: my Mentor Marcus Redfern insisted. He was my teacher since my young teens and I owed him much..."

I propped myself up, eager to hear what she wanted to share. I noticed our young Ranger hopeful was curious, too.

"After a couple of months at the castle learning everything I could, Marcus thought it wise to send me out on patrol along our perilous west border. I was one of five Rangers; my mates insisted I take the lead. We were out in the field for four days when we came upon a wagon. It was escorted by mounted warriors, sellswords, more accurately. Everyone in our group felt we should intercept and investigate. We planned to approach them along the roadway right before they were able to cross into Falnar's territory."

She walked around some and then continued, "And so we did. All our bows nocked, we took up the roadway, blocking their path. I demanded they explain their purpose, but they would have none of it and charged. So we fought. It was bloody and brutal.

Afterward, two of our own lay dead, along with all six sellswords. We were curious and baffled at what could be so bloody important to justify all this savagery, so we examined the wagon..."

She turned and looked at us. We were at full attention. I, for one, wanted to cherish this moment, because I knew not when it would happen again.

"We found they carried only one box. It was well secured, yet we broke through its lock..."

"What was in there?" Darna gasped, her youth and inquisitive nature showing through.

"We opened it... and found a large skull." Gadlynn said.

"A skull?" Darna puzzled, "Not jewels or gold?"

"Neither," Gadlynn replied. "It was very large. This- " She rapped again on the bone of the bear head, "put me in mind of it."

"Yet, this skull was fascinating. It was almost reptilian...

like the lizards in the swamps near Castin. Also... huge. You can criticize me all you care to, Monk, but I am convinced it was that of a dragon..."

"A dragon?" I replied, "I would need to thoroughly inspect before coming to that-"

"Of course you would. We all would, but it is not in our possession, for right as we discovered the skull, a contingent of troops- Falnar's troops- emerged upon us," Gadlynn replied, shaking her head at the memory of the encounter.

"We launched waves of arrows upon them, some occasionally finding their marks, but we were greatly outnumbered and knew we had to retreat. As we turned to run, a gigantic barbarian of a man pounced upon us from the treeline. We barely had time to react when he had swung his massive warhammer and killed a fellow Ranger. Jostin was his name... a good man, he was. As the barbarian swung at me, I dropped, evading the blow, but he followed through with his shield. His BEAR-head shield."

"Bear-head shield?" I interjected, "Sounds like it was none other than Wotan, Lavara's personal guard."

"I am convinced it was none other... that maggot." Gadlynn fumed.

"And then?" Darna coaxed.

"And then I saw a flash of light as his damnable shield connected with my head. It must have launched me ten feet into the forest. If not for the quick response and rescue of Third Ranger Flynn, I would have been a victim... a victim of a bear, another notch in the warhammer of Wotan."

I sat looking at her, realizing the pain and tragedy she must have faced, not only with that experience, but that of many others. It is a hard life these Rangers live.

“So as I stand here before you, as we look upon our conquest, I make a proclamation to the both of you: This will not be the last rabid bear that I partake in killing... there will be another. Wotan, I have not forgotten you; I have not forgotten the fouls deeds you did to my fellow Rangers. Someday, hopefully soon, there will be a reckoning.”

She stood there, proud and upright. Perhaps envisioning a worthy retribution delivered upon a stain that has brought only darkness to our world. Godspeed on that, Gadlynn. May your arrow swiftly find that monster’s heart.

“Record that in your journal, Monk. Let the histories prove

true my ability to follow through with a promise," Gadlynn said.

"After all this?" I waved my hands toward the beast. "And the story you just so uncharacteristically shared? My ink will constantly be running low through all the pages I scribe," I stated.

"Good. Now that we are rested, Darna, assist Matthew to the lair. I will check on the horses and get supplies. Do not enter without me," Gadlynn said.

"Very well, up with you now" Darna said, slipping her arm under my shoulder and helping me stand. My knee was beginning to swell; any movement instantly released a myriad of sharp pains. I could tell, being a master healer, that it would be some time before it was functioning normally again. Gadlynn disappeared into the dark of the forest. Darna and I carefully began our trek and (after only two slips onto my backside, I was proud to say) we made it all the way to the lair.

My leg throbbed in pain and convinced me to rest, so I sat upon some rocks. Sharp and jagged as they might be, my knee seemed unsympathetic to the desires of my backside. As I surveyed the surroundings of this cave... this "home" for this beast, my mouth gaped open in disbelief. I began to sort and absorb what I was viewing, trying ineffectively to comprehend this horrendous violation upon our world. And in complete revulsion, found I had to look away, so sickened was I by this ghastly environment. If not for the purpose of providing proof that this factually was the foul beast guilty of all the deaths and disappearances, I would not, for all of my lifetime, willingly gaze upon this unholy dwelling.

Now that we were able to view closer, it was clear that the bones riddling the ground near the entrance were mostly, unfortunately, human remains. The stench emitting from the opening was so wretched that it almost made me gag. Darna lifted a cloth to her nose, attempting to block the smell. I noticed tears swelling in her eyes, poor girl. To behold this atrocity and know it was the last dwelling of your own dear flesh and blood; my heart pained for her. So incredibly sad.

Gadlynn ran up carrying a large bag. She produced a flask of water from which I eagerly partook. One large axe was next, followed by two torches. She set about her flint and began striking, soon producing enough flame to ignite one of the torches. That, in turn, was used to light the other, which she offered to Darna.

"Are you sure you want to do this?" Gadlynn asked.

Darna did not respond aloud, just silently nodded her head. Gadlynn then looked to me, glanced down at my knee, and visually recommended I stay put and mend. I waved my hand, motioned for them to proceed without me. I will be just fine, sitting here not snooping around for evidence among half-rotted dead things inside that God forsaken Hell-hole. Yes, I will be just fine; on my backside, sitting, resting, warming this fine cluster of uncomfortable stones.

It did not take them as long as I expected. When the two returned, Darna immediately walked off to the side and proceeded to empty her stomach. Gadlynn approached me, and we stared at Darna briefly.

"How is it, with your ability to smell so spectacularly, that you are not next to her doing the same?" I questioned.

"Through practice, I've been able to stifle or... wall off scents that I do not want to smell, like yours for instance," Gadlynn replied.

"We just experienced- and lived through- and killed- one of the most lethal beasts to ever roam this earth... I feel I have earned the right to smell slightly unpleasant," I barked back.

"There is no 'slightly' about it," she replied smugly. That girl, even after this day's hard-fought battle, was still willing to pick a fight. Some among us are just geared for battle, I suppose.

"Perhaps you're right," I relented, then continued, "What is the axe for?"

She motioned over to where the beast lay. "Trophy. For the villagers."

"Proof," I nodded. "Evidence of its size and that it is truly dead. Makes sense. A bloody detail that will be. I would volunteer to help, if not for my knee..." I offered, attempting to receive some compassion yet knowing I would get none. I will take advantage of this injury as long as I am able. I feel I have earned the right not only to slightly smell yet also to bypass as unpleasant a task as the removal of the beast's head. It was I who landed the death blow!

"I'm sure you would," Gadlynn replied, not sounding at all convinced.

"Anything obvious inside? Cloths? Personal trinkets?" I asked.

"There was enough. I took what was necessary to prove without a doubt that the bear was guilty. The rest needs to remain... in this tomb. Do not ask me to go into further detail... it will haunt me forever."

"Fair enough," I said. Her being that distraught reminded me how grateful I was to not have had to go in there.

Darna walked over.

"I need to leave this foul place. It sickens me."

"Aye that," agreed Gadlynn. "It sickens us all. One final task and then we go home." She grabbed the sack of gear and motioned for Darna to once again assist me, being temporarily disabled and all. Through patience and cautious placement of each step, we soon arrived back at the site of the kill.

I saw the crossbow resting among ferns, shining with

contentment of a job well done. We will certainly retrieve that before leaving, I thought. Ambaum and Wils will insist on a full accounting of their handy work. Those two will receive nothing but adulation from me, that much is clear.

Gadlynn, axe in hand, walk toward the beast, intent on severing its head from its body. I was not sure I wanted to witness this; I've had enough of bloody, dire things for today- or any day for that matter.

Darna stood near me, stoic, emotionless, staring down at the monstrous brown bulk that lie before us. I noticed she mysteriously began to transform. Her demeanor changed, her countenance clouded, emotions swirling like a raging storm rekindling all the memories shared by her sister and using them to stoke the furnace of her wrath.

She began to tremble.

Gadlynn raised up to swing-

"NO!" Darna screamed.

Gadlynn paused, turning as Darna approached.

"No... let me..." The young woman pleaded. Gadlynn, being the wise Ranger she is, gave way and handed her the axe.

Darna approached the bear, positioned her feet close to its neck and looked down. Raising the axe high above her head, she brought it down, swift and hard. A bloody cleft lay open in its neck. The head still remain attached; it would take many strokes to decapitate a beast such as this.

She repositioned herself again and let the axe land, loosing a primal scream in the process.

Again she reeled up, striking downward, screaming, releasing months of anger, months of mourning, upon this creature's carcass.

Again and again, each time screaming louder, swinging harder, paying retribution upon this thief. This thief that violated the sanctity of her beloved family, stole from her a lifetime of shared laughs and loves and the joyful life that was to be shared with her sister.

With one final blow, the head detached from the beast's body.

She stood there, momentarily stunned, simply looking down upon a gruesome mess I won't even begin to describe. She threw the axe aside and promptly fell to her knees, her entire being consumed with emotion. Her hands went to her face and she began to wail uncontrollably.

Gadlynn turned and looked away. I bowed my head and found myself swept up in her grief. I could not help but join Darna with tears of my own.

***

The three of us were nearly back to Greensdale- thank you Good Lord. To look upon our party, a common traveler would probably laugh; the sight of us was something to behold. Mud, sweat, fur, dirt, blood, we wore it all... proudly. The incredibly large bear head hanging off the side of Blackwing grabbed the attention of a few and they, in turn, trotted off in the direction of the village, I am certain reporting the news of our party's success.

Hardly a word was said among us upon our ride back. Gadlynn returned to her usual self. Silent, guarded, focused, on exactly what I am not certain. Perhaps on how to deal most effectively with the Baron, making sure he honors his promise. Darna was understandably quiet, clearly recovering from the physically and emotionally- demanding experience.

Myself? My entire body ached. I must admit, I am getting older. My ability to recover swiftly from pains and injury is not high on my body's priority list and every step from Bitter remind me of just that. One incredibly hot bath was in order once we reach the Weary Woodsman, and it couldn't happen soon enough.

Rounding a bend in the road, we heard the clamor of people, as if a celebration were underway. We were eager to return and retire for the evening, so it was a relief knowing we were so close. I was then able to see the village up ahead, and it seemed as if the entire countryside was in attendance! It was not clear to me if it was a holiday exclusive to the village, or perhaps their beloved Baron was to speak.

We strolled inside the village as children ran around us pointing and laughing and even taunting the massive bear head at Gadlynn's side. Soon we were surrounded by throngs of villagers heaping upon our small party praise and cheer. All three of us were surprised at all the ruckus we even became slightly uncomfortable with all the attention. Never in my entire life did I expect to find myself in a situation such as this. Moments like these were meant for the famous, for Kings or Queens, the legendary knight in all his shining armor returning from a victorious battle.

The three of us were numb, as if in a dream, barely able to stay upright on our mounts. Despite our exhaustion, we continued forward, trotting our way into the thick of the throngs of celebration and experienced what most souls dream of and yet so very few ever obtain:

We rode in as heroes.

Someone in the crowd began chanting, "Ranger! Ranger!" and soon all joined along with its cadence. Gadlynn did her best to downplay all the acclamations and at times would point to both Darna and myself, attempting to deflect the praise our way. We would just nod. In complete honesty, we would have just preferred to return to our home or rooms and eagerly allow the sandman to lead us into a long, dreamless sleep.

We arrived in front of the inn, and before dismounting from our steeds (which would prove difficult with all the people), Gadlynn motioned for the crowd to quiet. After she had their attention, she spoke for all to hear.

"Good people of Greensdale, today is the day for you to celebrate the 'end'. The end of living in fear. The end of not knowing if you could wander out on your own lands, your own estates, after dark, for fear of being taken away into the night. This day, we celebrate the end of its reign of terror; we bring you proof... we bring you the head of this beast!" She struggled with the heavy trophy, but being so moved by the moment, Gadlynn hoisted the bear head for all to see- to see and witness the finality of this dark chapter in their town's history. As to be expected, the crowd loved every word the Ranger shouted and everything this moment meant for the security of their village and families. Wils and Ambaum stood among the crowd, adding cheers of their own. We sat upon our horses, basking in the grandeur of it all. This unexpected, dangerous course thrust upon us, and we came out the other side-

triumphant.

The crowd suddenly grew quiet. People began to move backward, allowing an opening in their midst to welcome the arrival of Baron Arlo and his entourage. The villagers looked at their leader adoringly, showering him with words of compliments. Yet his attention was fixed solely on Gadlynn as he walked forward, clapping his hands in an unusual rhythm, almost as if in mockery. The Baron's countenance radiated elegance and authority. It looked to me as if he was determined not to be outdone by the glory of our deed, to somehow direct the praise back his way. Eager ears awaited their Lord's response to this feat overcoming what had terrorized their town for so long...

"It is a mighty foe that you have defeated on this day!" declared the Baron. "A most remarkable... massive creature it is, yet I stand and wonder?"

"You bring us proof..." he continued. "That is well and good, yet still you have simply brought us proof of the end of *this* beast."

He stood, proud of his challenge, both congratulatory and contesting our claim all at once. I feel he seemed threatened not by our temporary love from the crowd, yet by the actual reality of him, the mighty Baron of Greensdale, forced to follow through with his commitment.

It was Darna who then surprised us all by speaking, "Most everyone here tonight knows me, and you know of the horror that my family has had to endure. I am not one to make up lies or falsehoods, especially dealing with this beast!" She swept her hand toward the bear's head.

"Now, now," soothed Baron Arlo. "No one is saying anyone is lying, just that you may be mistaken as to-"

"We explored," rang Darna's voice, rising above the Baron's patronizing words, "this nightmare's home... its lair." The crowd gasped and "ohh"s were heard throughout the throng.

"It was the most wicked site I have ever beheld. Bones scattered about the entrance. Animal remains would be expected for a bear, yet these bones were mostly human."

"I have verified that; it is true" I added. Again the crowd was horrified.

Darna continued, "Gadlynn and I entered in. Forever shall I be haunted by our discoveries..." She reached into a bag strapped upon her horse and produced a fistful of ragged scraps and trinkets. "Proof? Besides discovering human remains, we have these: a bit of tattered handkerchief with M.T. stitched inside-" A cry from within the crowd interrupted her, an older woman, a mother, perhaps, ran forward and took the cloth from Darna's hand.

"My Matty! Oh dear God... no..." Tears flowed down her face. She stood there trembling, holding the tattered cloth close to her heart, as if it were the last few moments with that of a dying loved one. Men walked forward and compassionately escorted her away.

"I am sorry for all that you have lost... retribution has been delivered." Tears forming in her eyes she continued, "I do not wish to display the rest of these. You can talk to me afterwards if you have need. I will only show this one last item." She held up a torn section of an embroidered shawl.

"This... this was my sister's. It took her weeks to make. She was so proud of it... she had it on the last night I saw her-" Darna held the cloth up to her face and began sobbing. Her parents ran up, and Darna slipped off her horse and embraced them. The crowd parted as Darna lead her horse through, and, arm in arm with her folks, consoling each other, she walked away without saying another word.

Gadlynn nudged Blackwing, pointing toward the Baron.

"You have your proof... without a doubt, this bear was the killer."

The audience agreed, adding voice of their own to her statement.

The Baron looked tense, slightly defensive, as if he considered countering our claim of guilt. But being the wise leader, the tactful politician that he is, saw the will of the crowd and adjusted his demeanor to fit.

He held out his hands for quiet, then began, "It seems the miraculous has happened. The terror that has plagued our people has been thwarted, defeated by our three heroes. In honor of their great deed, we shall celebrate tonight and tomorrow. Let this mark a new beginning in our town- our city's chapter: a beginning where we go forward without the fear of this beast haunting us. A beginning where Greensdale emerges as a prominent and bountiful city with endless possibilities for growth and status!"

In the praise and cheer that followed, the Baron held out his hands as if he were physically able to absorb their adulation.

He certainly knew how to shine bright and play a crowd, a gifted, natural leader and extremely charismatic. Yes, so very charismatic...I glanced over at Gadlynn, who in turn looked over at me. I instantly knew what was to follow. It was time to seal the agreement and fulfill our quest.

"The Baron has the right of it," Gadlynn declared. The people began to hush and listen once more. "It is a time of celebration, yet also that of mourning those who have fallen, those you have lost- to this foul beast. Let us continue forward in the hope of knowing that this beast is finally dead. And your town, or should I say, city, will begin a new journey of prosperity."

The people cheered and she went on, "I must bring attention to your most noble Baron Arlo." (More cheers!) "With his leadership, he oversaw our mission; he wholeheartedly approved of our undertaking, even offering the use of his troops to partake in the hunt. Most noble indeed. Now that the mission has proved successful, Baron Arlo- and your whole village- will begin to thrive in the upcoming years, with the construction of a new castle tower, stalwart protection even from an attack by Falnar's troops!"

The crowd erupted louder than before, carrying on excitedly.

Gadlynn continued, “So, as part of our agreement, witnessed by many good people here today, we bring you this bear’s head and the promise of a castle tower, in exchange for your... one little necklace.”

They clapped, feeling this bargain was certainly in their favor and eagerly looked to the Baron for a reply. Our part of the bargain fulfilled, there was no better time than the present to seek accountability of a presumed settled matter. Even knowing our agreement was going to be brought forth, he confused us by looking stunned, as if surprised at our audacity to ask for his necklace. He stood there, unmoving, his face clearly pained. It was apparent that inside his mind churned a fierce debate on whether to follow through or challenge, rejecting the agreement due to some insufficiency or another.

Yet, to our small party’s relief, slowly, his face began to transition from resistance to... guilt. Guilt, as if he were a child who had eaten the last bit of pie without permission, attempting to hide the crumbs that lie around his mouth- guilt as if he had willingly gained influence and acceptance from his people through unfair and artificial means.

Guilt. At times it burdens us all, for reasons large or small, and none of us are exempt. Our ability to accept and confess a wrong, a transgression, determines the outcome of the situation and the eventual shape of our character. This noble Baron was no exception; God is no respecter of person. We each stand individually before him, no special treatment due to nobility or status. Yet to his credit, Baron Arlo took the high path. A choice, I am glad to report, which will forever add depth and favor upon his history. Although he was shaking, he slowly reached back and unlatched the necklace. The years of security and comfort washed away as he removed the enchanted item. He looked down in shame, and I imagine that both of us shared a moment of wondering how his people will react to the real Jemson Arlo.

The real Baron Arlo now stood before them with no lustrous assistance from the false allure of enchantment.

The people were quiet, watching this special event unfold before them. They had no suspicions of hidden magical involvement, no accusations of the Baron taking advantage of their thoughts and emotions. They were oblivious to the entirety of the moment, not a hint of the enormity being played out.

Gadlynn, with incredible intuition and foresight, might I add, quickly slipped from Blackwing and walked over to the Baron. She held out her hand, inside hoping, perhaps praying, that he follow through with his commitment.

She stood in front of him, hand open, for what felt like quite a while. The Baron continued to look down, holding the necklace tightly in his hand. As I looked upon him, I had the impression he was settling the finality of this matter in his mind, his heart, as if saying his goodbyes to a lover or the dearest of friends. Then, to the relief of us all (mostly the two of us,) he reached out and turned his palm over, dropping the necklace into her hand.

The crowd roared with approval.

Gadlynn drew a deep breath, her relief was evident. Without hesitation she placed the necklace into one of her pockets. In the absence of its magical charm, the Baron continued to stare downward, afraid to look upon his people, perhaps afraid they may witness some kind of instant horrific transformation, as if he were a raving monster prior to the necklace. But the villagers knew not what the Ranger and I did. They did not even consider to watch as his grand allure began to dissipate. His proud-bearing facade was stealthily crumbling, returning to that of a normal good-hearted man struggling with his own self-doubt and insecurities. Again, as of now, they were oblivious to any erosion of beauty displayed in their Baron. The villagers were unsuspecting; they simply wanted to continue in celebration. The dreaded beast was dead.

Our First Ranger, again to her credit, recognized that the Baron, rather than looking triumphant, more resembled a man defeated. Before the masses could take notice, she seized their attention once more, shouting, “Good people of Greensdale, hear me once again!” They instantly simmered down and listened.

“I want to remind you, to bring attention to something you already know, yet something worth repeating while we are all gathered.” She turned her complete focus upon the Baron. “Before us stands a man you proudly declare your leader, Baron Arlo.” (Cheers followed.) “You have seen his good deeds on full display, and they are highly commendable. When I return to King Gerald, I will be eager to tell him about the town of Greensdale and the fine quality of its people. But I will also be eager to share about the noble character of this man. The man who followed through on an agreement, a pact of great importance. A man who, when he gave his word, honored his word and followed through on his promise. Your leader, Baron Arlo!”

The people of Greensdale shouted, praising the Baron’s name. I was curious if the villagers would soon lose their voices from all the cheering, though I was pleased to see it continue on.

Gadlynn pulled the Baron in close, almost an embrace and whispered into his ear, “You have it from here.”

She nodded to him knowingly, implying directly that he could proceed in honor without help from any sorts of magic, tempting though they may be. She then pulled away, walked back to her horse, quickly mounted Blackwing, and we carefully rode off through the thickness of humanity, delivering an occasional wave and smile and of course plenty of "your welcome"s.

It seemed that her thoughtful words rekindled a flame in the Baron's heart, for he lifted his head high, rose up with new hope, shining and basking in the celebration of this most victorious and glorious night. It was a new beginning in so many different ways. The beast was now dead and new development would soon follow, along with additional, most-welcomed population and prosperity.

(As time went on, the people continued to receive him warmly).

Still, the lack of appeal and fondness they had developed for him would slowly recede with time. They could not know, nor recognize why they had been so enamored with him in the first place, but at least it would happen in a way that was natural and organic.

- The Baron lived long and happy and received nothing different than that of the same fate of every person of prominence and leadership, eventually you lose it, eventually the people change course and take it from you or you retire. He chose to retire.

It is the way our world works, it is human nature.

- After breaking through the crowd, Gadlynn and I rode the short distance to the inn. We dismounted and made sure Bitter and

Blackwing were thoroughly care for. They had served us extraordinarily well. Florence was glad to see me, and this made me smile. I was unable to reward her dedication to my happiness with a fresh apple; however, I did find a large bundle of carrots. She offered no complaints, and did not even notice when I walked away and retreated back into the inn. After a meal or three, void of any significant conversation, I parted ways with the Ranger, and we promptly returned to our rooms to retire for the evening. My nightly journal entries would have to wait; I was physically done. I was immensely pleased to notice a hot bath was prepared and waiting upon my arrival. I shall not disappoint this unexpected preparation! After everything my body and I have experienced on this monumental day, I eagerly disrobed and entered.

I had just submerged into the waters of Heaven itself.

My hostess will absolutely be receiving an impressive and substantial gratuity upon my departure. I lay there, soaking in the glory of soap and steamy hot water, encouraging my body to begin its healing process and actually attempt to welcome some recently unfamiliar sensations, like that of... comfort. I do believe that if my knee could talk, it would- then and there verbally thank me for getting my large frame off of it. Small wonder it is, the effect of hot, beautiful water on a tired, bruised old man. I found myself reaching for another glass of wine, and, after the gratification of its draining, I discovered I had no available means of fighting off sleep. I soon drifted into the vast, uncharted plains of dreams, in the midst of dirty bath water.

So be it.

* * *

The following day, around noon- the Ranger and I could easily claim we were guilty of being sluggards for sleeping in so late. Honestly, I could have slept another four hours without any trouble if not for the irresistible smell of bacon and fried eggs being prepared on our account. Though my body protested, my stomach did not and I arose, washed, dressed and met our valiant Ranger out in the main hall of the inn. The breakfast was fabulous, the conversation not so much; once again she returned to that reserved and constrained enigma. She offered me no additional notes or thoughts that I might add to my journal upon our return. The Ranger was quite a different sort, I have come to learn. She has purposely built walls around her for some reason or another, and I am not to judge that. Despite my struggle to be irritated at her silent mannerisms, I must remind myself that this is her way, this is who she is.

I wouldn't change it for the world.

That afternoon both the First Ranger and I spent a good long while talking with Wils and Ambaum. Reliving the trails of yesterday, that nightmare we would soon rather forget if it were not so impacted upon our memories. They deserved a thorough accounting for all the effort they put forth. Good people they are.

After many goodbyes, we rode toward the Mt. Goor pass, but first we had a little stop at a certain farmhouse along the way. It was the Deloom homestead. We had a comforting conversation over lunch with Darna and her parents. It was apparent that they were still in the process of mourning, and, out of respect, we did our best to keep the talk light and steer the mood toward the positive. Greensdale certainly had a way of producing good folk; Darna and her parents were fine examples of that. Right before our departure, I was pleasantly surprised to receive a long and heart-felt hug from Darna. She even gave our First Ranger one, awkward though it was. You have probably gathered by now that Gadlynn is just not one for physical affection. She did, however, hand Darna a scroll, concerning what I know not, nor do I feel it is my place to ask. It appeared to be a private matter.

With pleasant weather, we said our goodbyes, and, come nightfall, wouldn't you know it? We had no choice but to camp close to the lair. I care not to look upon that unholy tomb ever again, and even being this near was disheartening, but sleep was welcoming. The bright, warm roar of the fire gave us a feeling of security- more for myself than her I am certain- but it was comforting.

After three days of travel, we had returned to the castle.

Chapter 15

FINAL THOUGHTS

Again, the four of us found ourselves seated around that impressive, large table that filled the center of the King's study. The good King Gerald and Adviser Galvanster were curiously festive; perhaps the lunch wine was uncommonly potent, or perhaps they were overjoyed at the "gift" of a certain necklace Gadlynn presented. Either way, it was well to be back and see the mood was upbeat. So often times, in this setting, the atmosphere was dark, filled with talk of war and strategies how best to combat our enemies.

"And then the blasted thing just turned around and bit me!" I exclaimed, retelling the tale of my horse and its appetite for monk leg. "Left a massive bruise I might add..." I'm thankful it didn't prefer breast meat."

"I warned you dear Brother," guffawed the King, holding back mirthful tears, "DO NOT fool with its ears!" They all were laughing at my accounting of my dear mount and its sensitivity with its ears. Even Gadlynn was smirking, whether out of courtesy of the company or entertaining thought of me experiencing pain, I was not sure. I continued, “After that incident, I thought the horse sour indeed. Whoever had named him, named him well. Bitter... ha!” I jested, but it seemed the joke was on me, for the King and Adviser shared a puzzled look before erupting in laughter.

“Bitter? Where did you hear that? His name is Biter! ” King Gerald said.

Of all the...

“That half brained lackey of a guard told me his name was Bitter... ahh!” I replied in frustration. They all seemed to be highly amused.

“Now, now,” said King Gerald. “He might be severely hard-headed, but he is dedicated.”

“Who? The horse or the soldier?”

“Both, I am certain,” laughed the King, then continued on in a more serious tone, “I am most grateful for your dedication to the task. The both of you and the good folks from Greensdale are to be commended. I will send designers soon to help the Baron plan for a new castle tower. It is a very strategic location; with the barracks so close, it makes perfect sense to fortify the area.”

“That was my thought also,” I added. “I am pleased you see it the same.”

“I do,” affirmed the King. “I look forward to your full report, your journal of the quest. I imagine it will be quite the entertaining and sobering read."

"My ink and quill are at your service, my King."

"Very well, you two go to your homes or quarters and rest, relax. This quest is officially ended. Yet know this: I have many more awaiting, so do not become too accustomed to idleness."

"I am ready now, if need be, my King" Gadlynn said. She was quite serious, ready to go out this very instant, back into the wilds. Ahh, to be young again- I have forgotten what that was like.

"I am certain you are, Gadlynn. But for now," Gerald stated, "go see to your Rangers. Then, afterward, you rest."

He stood. We followed his lead, then we all bowed to him, and he, back to us. I am so fortunate to serve him and not that of the wicked Falnar- the thought of that is unbearable.

The King exited, followed by Adviser Galvanster. Gadlynn made for the door and proceeded down the hallway. I was close behind, yet her stride separated us rapidly. Seems she had no time for idle chit chat. That is all well and good; I must force myself to be content with her choice to be reclusive. Yet then she surprised me: before rounding the hallway and disappearing from my sight, she turned to me and said, "Matthew..."

"Yes, Gadlynn?" I curiously replied.

"About our little quest. Not too bad... for a monk."

"Not too bad... for a Ranger," I instantly replied.

She shined a hint of a smile and rounded the corner, disappearing until I saw her again, which was soon enough.

Small favors? The good Lord just gave me one in the form of a semi-kind word and gesture from one thick-skulled, divinely gifted Ranger.

Our world will never cease to amaze me.

***

Surrounded by scrolls and writing implements, I labored away, noting rapidly the thoughts that had been filling my mind. It was sobering indeed, some of the recounting of our adventure. Yet it was also gratifying, knowing that through great effort and persistence, our party of three, my comrades and I, still remain upon this grand world for at least a little while longer. Hopefully to continue on that path we have chosen- or in my case, directed by the Almighty to follow.

My flow of words was interrupted by an annoying knock upon my door.

RAP RAP RAP!

Ahhh... what is it now?? I put my quill down and attended to the inquiry. Standing there was the last royal guard I ever wanted to see. The one gifted with a wide divide of emptiness between his ears.

"Yes?" I said, attempting to be decent.

He was having none of it. Once again, his arrogant tone suffocated any attempt at a rational course of civility.

"You have returned," he said, with an air of disappointment. "I will see the horse back to its proper stall."

"I was under the impression that the King would have me keep him?" I probed, "Has there been a misunderstanding of sorts?" I did my best to be calm, yet wanted to explode inside.

"This has not been brought to my attention. I will return the creature at once," the guard demanded.

I did my best to remain composed, though difficult it was. I will take this matter up with the King himself.

"Fine, do with... BITTER... what you must," I replied, perhaps a bit too sternly, yet, in the heat of the moment, I cared not.

"I shall," he said, "and I will." He then abruptly turned and headed for the stall.

"Oh!" I said, helpfully requesting his attention.

"What?" he replied.

"In case you find him a bit stubborn and hesitant to move, you might want to try tickling his ears... he is quite fond of it. It works every time," I offered.

I shall pray for him. On second thought...perhaps I won't.

I closed the door and sat back down, once again partaking

of the laborious task before me. I was pleased to notice that my hands remained mostly that of my normal skin tone and not the black of spilled ink. This was good.

Then I heard the most welcoming, pleasant sound of a pained scream piercing the air. Ahhh... Biter found his mark.

I smiled wide, grateful that a little retribution has just been distributed.

Good Lord forgive me; at times I am such a disobedient servant.

***

Later that evening I found myself, once again, soaking in heavenly hot waters inside of a large, wooden tub. I am glad to say that this session was not in some unfamiliar inn room but back in my quaint, humble abode. Candles lit the room; their calm, orange flicker and pleasing aroma greeted my senses warmly. The atmosphere was exactly what was needed. My body was beginning to heal, complete with fully functioning knees, I might add. I reached out and drained the last of the fine vintage that remained in my glass, welcoming the sudden rush of numb mixed with a dash of contentment. This was the life.

I just sat there, pondering what I had just experienced and what could possibly be in store for my future. The more I gave it thought, the more I was of the opinion that it was out of my control, so I just surrendered it all to my heavenly Father. One thing is for certain: my future road is intertwined with you-know-who. Just the thought of this made me reach out and pour another glass. Ah, yes... Gadlynn. It was difficult to imagine the potential, the abilities- so many different ways she could possess and control them if she would only reach out and accept her "gift". That confusing, yet wonderful, "higher calling" of hers.

Embrace it, Gadlynn. Throw your anger and reservation aside, and embrace it fully. Become that beacon of hope, that warrior of truth and righteousness!

Embrace it, I pray.

Again, I am in no position to judge. Her story remains unfinished, and I am certain that plenty of pages will be filled in journals concerning her history, the many fascinating tales that are yet untold.

I look forward to writing them.

Yet, it is an easy position, and a cowardly one, to sit back and witness what another is doing- right or wrong- in their life, and be determined to convey your thoughts on how they could better themselves if they would only heed your advice. I must remind myself to not be prey to this trap, this fallacy. It is beneath us.

In Gadlynn Wayfare's situation, I will continue to remember to hold my tongue, keep my opinions to myself. This will prove to be difficult; that girl is about as stubborn as a mule unwilling to move or that raging Infantry Sergeant training new recruits... or the old monk convinced his ways are always the best ways.

Guilty.

I shall not judge. I know not what it be like to face what she has, and what she will. I do not walk in her boots.

Yet I am very pleased to say-

-that I walk beside them.

Chapter 16

EPILOGUE -

An unexpected rain poured. Wind swept fiercely on what was supposed to be a pleasant early-summer evening. The foul weather made the darkness near impossible to see through, yet the rider was determined and continued forward. The road eventually lead true and the destination was present: a long row of barracks and a grand gathering hall. Eager to be free of this perpetual downpour, perhaps even to warm oneself by the fireside, the rider quickly dismounted, tied off their mount and walked to the large wooden door of the main entrance.

The sign next to the door was not finely decorative nor elaborate. It was plainly carved, only serving its purpose of announcing "The King's Rangers - Training Hall". The stranger was relieved, their destination finally before them.

BOOM BOOM BOOM.

Three hard knocks produced an almost instant result. Fourth Ranger Korsten opened the door widely, neither afraid nor suspicious of the stranger who stood before him. He wore a dark brown vest of studded leather. A tidy half-beard adorned his chin.

His face was chiseled, and his body the same. Korsten measured the person in front of him, not knowing how to evaluate, for a large, gray cloak and a stormy evening concealed the stranger entirely.

"Yes?" Korsten asked.

"I have a message to deliver," the stranger replied. It was neither courteous nor sharp in tone, only direct.

"Is it important?"

"It is to me".

He took the note, stepped back from the doorway under a light, unrolled the scroll and read its contents. Korsten turned and faced his fellow Rangers behind him.

"It's from Gadlynn," he announced.

Others quickly walked forward. A tall, lanky Ranger asked, "What does it say?"

Korsten eyed the stranger before him, this time with more respect.

"She says, 'The person bearing this note is to be accepted into Ranger training immediately and will be received as one of our own. Darna Deloom has more than proven her worthiness. Signed, Gadlynn Wayfare, First Ranger of the King.'"

The Rangers were impressed. Korsten quickly added, "You're Darna, I presume?"

“None other,” she said, removing the cowl and revealing her handsome face and braided blonde hair.

“Well then, come inside, get yourself out of the rain. We will get you some supper- I suppose you’re hungry?” he asked.

“Very,” Darna admitted.

“I hope you like bean stew.”

“I will take what is given me.”

“That’s the right of it; come along, follow me. Your training begins first thing in the morning,” he said as she entered and he closed the door behind her.

In a male-dominated class of elite warriors such as the prestigious King’s Rangers, female involvement was almost unheard of. Yet it was through Gadlynn’s victory at a monumental tournament and her continued efforts that opened up an opportunity for this chance to even exist or even be considered.

Darna Deloom’s dream was now in the process of becoming a reality. She began her training and would soon elevate her position through hard work and dedication. Darna was determined to make her parents proud, to bring them honor and respect, yet also to honor the fond memory of her dear sister, Alena, who will forever live in her heart.

Thank you for joining us on this tale of adventure!

Stay tuned for our next book:

"Gadlynn Wayfare and the Red Fiddle of Fire"

David L. Anderson

About the author-

Photo by Douglas Herring

At an early age David filled much of his time immersed in monster movies, comic books and fantasy reading. After growing up, his love for these genres have not changed, only expanded. Dave now enjoys composing music, writing and producing independent film and authoring books – that is of course when he is not as his day job.

He resides in the Seattle area and would love to hear from you and correspond. You can reach him at dl.anderson@comcast.net.

Please like "First Ranger of the King" on Facebook and stay tuned for the next book,

Gadlynn Wayfare and the Red Fiddle of Fire!

–expected in 2020.

LINKS:

https://www.imdb.com/name/nm4922512

https://www.facebook.com/1stRangerOfTheKing

http://firstrangeroftheking.com

Made in the USA
Monee, IL
19 July 2020